EARL GREY AND SHALLOW GRAVES

A WATERWHEEL CAFE MYSTERY

VICTORIA TAIT

KANGA PRESS

Cover Design by Daniela Colleo of StunningBookCovers.com
Editing Allie Douglas

For more information visit VictoriaTait.com

Find Keya's Chocolate Chip Cookie recipe,
and her notes about Earl Grey tea at the back of this book.

CHAPTER ONE

Sergeant Keya Varma smiled to herself as she drove her speedy Ford Focus police car through the narrow Cotswold lanes. England in late spring was glorious.

The green leaves of the beech hedges on either side of the road were fresh and vibrant. Even the large oak trees, which in winter stood like elderly sentinels, were covered in new buds and, as she glanced at one, pollen dispersed into the air as a breeze ruffled the long strands of male catkins.

Spring was a time for renewal and fresh starts. Which is exactly what she was doing.

The Rural, Heritage and Wildlife Unit she had worked for had been disbanded and the Chief Inspector who ran it officially retired. But he, and Keya as a member of his team, had been subjected to questioning, and investigated for corruption, embezzlement, and involvement in a local antique scam.

Keya had been cleared, which was only reasonable since she had been one of the group that had exposed the chief inspector. He'd exchanged a police cell for his comfortable retirement only by giving evidence against the ringleader of the group behind the antiques fraud.

As Keya had been working closely with the local community in the Cotswolds, she'd been appointed Rural Engagement Officer, which sounded far more important than it was. There wasn't even a budget for her role to be full-time, but that also suited her, as she was planning to open a cafe at Akemans, a local antiques centre and auction house.

Although she enjoyed her job, being caught up in the antique scam and sidelined to minor roles had left her feeling disheartened and rather jaded with her police work. She had always dreamed about opening a local cafe and deli so she was excited about her new Waterwheel Cafe.

But before she stopped in at Akemans to see how the building and renovation work was progressing, she'd been invited by the inhabitants of Coln Akeman, only half a mile from the antiques centre, to their May Day festivities.

An old stone animal trough at the entrance to the village was brimming with wild flowers, including clusters of yellow cowslips, some delicate deep-pink flowers and, behind them, tall foxgloves adorned with purple bell-shaped flowers.

The festival had attracted many visitors to the village, and Keya had to park several hundred metres away from the central village green, at the end of a line of other parked cars.

The green was wedge-shaped, with its shortest side beside the River Coln, after which the village was named. The road through the village ran along the broader side, lined by The Axeman pub, the village post office, and a row of houses built from Cotswold's iconic honey-coloured stone, all overlooking the green.

"Morning Sergeant," an elderly man greeted Keya. He was wearing a flat tweed cap and leaning against a wooden gate at the entrance to his small front garden. "You'll be here to mark the beginning of summer, then?"

"I am, and I'm particularly looking forward to seeing the maypole dancing."

"So are other folk." He scowled at the gathering crowd on the green.

"Now, Bob, none of that negative talk," chided a plump woman wearing a white apron with green teapots printed on it and 'The WI' in large letters. Keya knew this stood for The Women's Institute, a popular organisation bringing women together for friendship and offering them a place to make a difference in their community.

"Visitors spend money at the pub, and don't forget the WI are serving teas, coffees and cakes."

The WI were fiercely proud of their reputation as expert bakers.

"And we should embrace our village traditions." The woman added.

"Aye, well, May Day was originally a Roman tradition where daft soldiers danced around trees in homage to their goddess Flora and the arrival of spring."

"You do come out with some! I've no idea where you heard th… "

"Radio 4," muttered Bob.

"But our celebration is for the arrival of summer," emphasised the woman with a sharp nod.

"And it certainly feels like it," agreed Keya, pleased she'd decided not to wear her heavy black police jacket.

She was about to walk away when the plump lady called, "Mind you try one of my chocolate chip cookies!"

Keya smiled at her before walking on.

Part of Keya's role was to provide police visibility in rural communities, which, in turn, was meant to reassure residents. But rural crimes were on the rise and as she was the only Rural Engagement Officer in the Cotswolds, she was unable to deal with all the thefts of agricultural equipment, fly-tipping, and vandalism.

Women, and a few men, all dressed in white, had gathered around the tall maypole which had been erected on the green. They stood in pairs, each holding the end of a coloured ribbon, with the other end attached to the top of the maypole.

A man on the other side of the maypole, with a straggly grey beard and tartan cap, had a red accordion strapped across his front. He hit the keys on one side of it, which resembled a small piano, pushed in buttons on the other side, and tapped his foot as he pushed the bellows together to make music sound.

This traditional folk music was the signal for the pairs of dancers to weave in and out of each other around the maypole and, as they did, the ribbons on the white pole crossed each other. As the lengths of ribbon shortened, the dancers moved closer to the pole until it was covered in a multicoloured patchwork.

The music stopped, and the crowd, including Keya, applauded.

She moved towards two trestle tables and realised this was the WI stall. Once caught in the beady stare of another apron-wearing woman, she had no choice but to approach it.

"What can I get you?" asked the lady, her voice edged with the local Gloucestershire burr.

"Erm" Keya regarded the packs of scones and plates of brownies and oatie flapjack. The lady was moving her hand towards a large chocolate cake, so Keya asked hastily, "Do you have any chocolate chip cookies?"

With a brief tightening of the lips, the woman moved along the table and picked up a plastic bag of cookies. "That'll be £5."

Keya had only wanted one, but under the woman's steely gaze she didn't protest and handed over a five-pound note in exchange for the cookies. Maybe the builders at the Waterwheel Cafe construction site would enjoy them.

CHAPTER TWO

Keya returned to her car and drove slowly through the village, navigating her way around groups of lingering visitors, and out towards Akemans antiques centre and auction house.

The antiques centre occupied a converted three-storey, nineteenth century flour mill, and the auction house a single-storey stone building beside it. Other stone storage buildings, warm and mellow in the sunlight, surrounded the gravel parking area. There were a number of cars, but her friend Dotty's green Skoda was conspicuously absent from the staff parking spaces at the front.

Dotty, who Keya considered her best friend, was taking a break in France, looking after the twin daughters of a former antique dealer. They had worked on a number of cases together, even though Dotty was a civilian.

But during their last one, Dotty had been arrested by Keya's colleague, Sergeant Nick Unwin. A combination of the arrest, the realisation that she'd been working closely with the antique gang's ringleader, and an attempt on her life, had left Dotty exhausted.

As Keya's sturdy black shoes crunched across the gravel, she considered the closed auction house door with a sense of loss and an ache in her chest. She hoped Dotty wouldn't stay away too long.

Skirting the edge of the auction house, she followed a makeshift track created by the builders' vehicles to the rear of the antiques centre. An area of ground at the side of the centre, which extended down to the edge of the River Coln, had already been landscaped and was a mixture of grass and patches of bare brown earth. Keya planned to use part of it as an outdoor seating area.

Lengths of string marked out the foundation trenches, some of which had already been dug, for a single-storey building which would be her office and gift shop.

A rough arch shape had been knocked out of the antiques centre's side wall, where a pair of double glass access doors would be installed later. But what she was most excited about was the renovation of the flour mill's wooden waterwheel, and the creation of floor to ceiling height windows in the back wall, giving customers a view of what she hoped would be a working version of the wheel.

"Morning, Sergeant," greeted Vic Peters, the foreman, as he tipped his yellow plastic hard hat at her. He handed her a similar one and a high-vis vest, which she pulled on over her police uniform.

"I thought you might like these. I bought them in the village at the May Day festivities." Keya handed over the plastic bag of chocolate chip cookies from which she'd already removed one, just so she could taste it. For research purposes, of course.

"Brad," Vic called to a man with his back to them, working at the top of the slope which led down to the riverbank. Brad turned, put down his hammer and walked towards them, navigating a double line of scaffolding planks placed across an area of muddy ground.

Brad was older than the other men on the construction site and tufts of grey hair protruded from under his yellow hard hat.

Vic handed him the bag of cookies and said, "Share these amongst the lads."

To Keya, Vic said, "Brad's a good influence on the boys."

Brad gave a lopsided smile as he replied, hesitantly, "We were all young and excitable once and did things we regretted." His voice was soft and with a trace of an accent she couldn't place.

"Speak for yourself," retorted Vic. "I'm not that old, and neither is the sergeant."

Brad shrugged and turned towards the mill building.

"Just a minute," called Vic.

Brad turned back as Vic said to Keya, "I'm glad you popped by. The waterwheel team have confirmed they're coming tomorrow. At least, that's what they told Brad. Can't be doing with them myself. All this new age mumbo jumbo and turning up when they like. They've already added a week to the schedule faffing about. That's why I've tasked Brad to deal with them. He has more patience than me."

Brad nodded. "Rowan assured me his team will be here by half past eight in the morning."

Rowan Cartwright, which Keya thought a highly suitable name for a man who specialised in restoring wooden buildings, vehicles, and items of heritage, liked to take his time, and could even be described as pernickety.

He'd been fussing for several weeks over the dismantling and removal of the waterwheel, and insisting Vic and his men reinforce the wall, preventing river water from flowing down the waterwheel's dedicated channel.

It was clear from the trees, grass, and wild plants growing in the channel, and around the waterwheel, that it hadn't been used for years.

Vic pulled at his chin and replied, "If they don't mess around, we might be able to pull back some of the lost time."

That was good, thought Keya, who knew that any delays completing the building and restoration work would push back the opening day for the cafe, currently scheduled for mid-June, the week after her younger sister's wedding.

Keya followed Vic and Brad into the mill building to view the renovation work and construction of the kitchen and new toilet block.

"Keya! Checking up on the work?" cried Gilly Wimsey, who ran the antiques centre. She was a motherly type with a bright smile and even brighter orange hair which hung in ringlets around her face.

She tucked one unruly ringlet behind her ear as she approached Keya and remarked, "It's looking good in here, isn't it? I can't wait to see what it'll be like once the opening is created in the outside wall and the large windows are installed."

The space where they were standing had been stripped back so its Cotswold stone walls, stone-flagged floor, and wooden beams and ceiling planks were all exposed.

"A cafe is a much better use of this space than antique stalls, and now a breeze block wall has been erected between here and the main sales area, the stallholders have stopped moaning, and some are even excited about it, and the new toilets."

Keya wondered if their enthusiasm was directed in that order. She replied, "And Vic has confirmed that they've strengthened the channel wall so Rowan and his team should begin tomorrow."

Gilly wandered out of the building and Keya followed her until they both stopped and looked across at the waterwheel. Its wooden paddles were green with moss, and some rotten ones had collapsed onto lower panels.

"My friends and I used to climb down onto that bridge when we were young," Gilly said. She indicated towards a narrow stone bridge across the end of the waterwheel channel, which connected the channel's stone wall with the riverbank.

"And jump off it into the river. Where the bank is eroded, after the waterwheel channel, there's a shallow pool which was a great place to splash around on balmy summer days. Sometimes Aunt Beanie would bring us cakes and cold drinks, or ice creams, when she took a break from running the auction house."

Keya had worked with Gilly's Aunt Beanie, whose full name was Bernadette Devereux, in The Rural, Heritage and Wildlife Unit. But she had also lost her consultant's position when the unit was disbanded. She was now working with a local company assessing collections of paintings and arranging exhibitions for local artists.

Gilly was still lost in the past as she mused, "I miss those days. And my friends."

"What happened to them?" Keya asked politely.

"Katherine moved away and Rachael … well, never mind. So the work on the wheel should start in the morning?"

Keya, wondering about Gilly's unusual reticence to speak about her childhood friends, replied, "Fingers crossed."

CHAPTER THREE

That evening, Keya closed the door of her end-of-terrace house in the attractive Cotswold village of Ampney St Martin, five miles east of the historic town of Cirencester, looking forward to the evening ahead.

Unlike most Cotswold properties, hers was brick rather than local stone and she'd been told it was built as part of the government's social housing policy in the 1950s.

"Popping down to the pub?" called her neighbour and landlady, Peggy, over the trim boxwood hedge which separated their front gardens. Peggy and her husband, Derek, had moved into their property in 1971 when they'd married, and Derek had taken a job on a local farm.

They told Keya they'd bought her house from a friend, after his wife died and he moved away to live with his daughter, as they didn't want any 'nouveau riche townies' moving in who didn't understand country ways.

"Yes, I'm meeting a couple of friends," Keya called back.

"If you see my Derek, can you make sure he leaves by nine. He's taking me for a hospital appointment tomorrow."

"Nothing serious, I hope?" enquired Keya.

"No, no. Nothing to worry about." Peggy shook her head vigorously and Keya felt she wasn't being entirely truthful.

Keya loved her little house and being part of the community, but Derek and Peggy were in their 70s and she knew that at some point in the not-too-distant future they would want to sell her snug two-bed house, and perhaps their own. Joined together, their homes would make a desirable larger property.

She'd been saving up, but the amount was unlikely to be enough to buy in such a popular location. And now she was using some of those savings to start her cafe. Still, she'd enjoy living here whilst she could.

The Dog and Duck pub was where the locals congregated and it served what it referred to as 'bar meals' rather than the fancy food of the Coach and Horses, the other pub in the village, fronting the main road to Cirencester.

She pushed open the door and spotted her friends sitting at a table in the corner, close to the unlit fireplace. She crossed the stripped wooden floor onto the Indian rug, the vibrant reds and golds of it having faded from many years of wear and spilt drinks.

"Hiya, sorry I'm late," announced Keya.

Ryan looked up from a bench formed from the slatted wooden panels which ran along the entire wall of the room at waist height and gave her a boyish smile. He was the youngest and most junior member of the team Keya now worked with, but he was also one of the brightest, especially when it came to technical matters and computers.

"I like your local," he declared.

"Is this the first time you've been here?" asked Keya.

"Yes. Although my parents have taken me to the Coach and Horses for Sunday lunch."

Keya glanced across at Ozzie Winters, sitting on the opposite side of the rectangular, dark-wood table. Her spiky black hair was even shorter than when Keya had last seen her, when they'd discovered a collection of paintings, many of which had been illegally acquired, in the loft rooms of a large Cotswold house.

"I used this place as an example of traditional pubs in the Cotswolds for one of my articles," explained Ozzie, who was a reporter for the Cirencester Times. She was young, probably not even twenty, but keen and enthusiastic, and she had written some interesting pieces about the last few cases Ryan and Keya had worked on.

"Anyone for a drink?" asked Keya.

"I'd love a vodka and tonic," Ozzie replied.

"A pint of zero or low alcohol beer, please," said Ryan.

Keya moved across to the bar at the back of the room.

"What can I get you?" asked Kate, the barmaid who was on duty. She had a sing-song Scottish accent which was pleasant to listen to and not as difficult to understand as some Scots, particularly those Keya had met from Glasgow.

"Do you have any low alcohol beer?" asked Keya.

"I'm glad you asked," smiled Kate, tucking a strand of shoulder-length blonde-streaked hair behind her ear. Keya noticed that one of her fingers was crooked. Kate must have noticed her staring at it as she said, "Accident as a child. Now, I've just persuaded Coll, the landlord, to stock low alcohol beers. We have Becks Blue or BrewDog Nanny State."

"Oh, the BrewDog sounds interesting."

As Kate reached into a glass-fronted fridge at the back of the bar, Keya tried, as she had done previously, to judge Kate's age. Her face was lined with several small scars and her skin had a grey tinge. Keya guessed she was in her fifties. But her eyes were bright and intelligent.

Keya didn't drink herself. She'd been brought up a Hindu and although she rarely visited a temple, she still adhered to many of the practices, including abstaining from drinking alcohol, and not eating meat.

She thanked Kate and carried Ozzie and Ryan's drinks over to the table, then returned for her own orange juice and lemonade.

"Are you eating?" asked Kate, waving a paper menu at her. "Only, it's Coll's sister standing in today and she needs to leave early, so last orders for food will be in …" She glanced up at the large round wall clock at the far end of the bar. "Twenty minutes."

"Definitely, I'm starving." Keya grabbed three single-sheet menus and carried them across to her table with her drink.

"I'll come over and take your order," Kate called after her.

Keya passed menus to Ryan and Ozzie as she explained that they needed to decide what they wanted to eat before the kitchen closed.

"When I visited in the autumn, I tried the steak and kidney pudding as part of my research for an article I was writing on local pub food," offered Ozzie. "It's excellent, as long as you like kidneys."

"I might try that, then," said Ryan, "with mashed potatoes and seasonal veggies, but there isn't a vegetarian option for you." He looked across at Keya as she removed her coat and sat down next to Ozzie.

"Don't worry, they're used to me here, and will make me something from whatever they have to hand."

"I'm going to try the Hunters Chicken. I don't remember seeing it on the menu before," declared Ozzie.

"What is it?" asked Ryan.

"A chicken breast wrapped in bacon, served in a BBQ sauce, and topped with melted cheese. And it's served with chips, which is exactly what I feel like this evening."

Kate appeared at their table and asked, "Found anything you fancy tonight?" She raised an eyebrow at Ryan.

Ryan's cheeks flushed as he replied, "I've been recommended the steak and kidney pudding."

"Excellent choice," agreed Kate, making a note on a small pad.

Ozzie was considering Kate as she said, "You weren't here when I wrote about the pub?"

Kate smiled pleasantly and explained, "I started just before Christmas, when I moved back to the area and Coll was short-staffed and agreed I could help out. And he seems happy enough with my work." She lowered her voice and added, "Happy enough that he's taken his wife to Majorca for two weeks and left me in charge."

Keya glanced around. It was a Tuesday evening and only a handful of regulars were drinking in the pub.

Keya recognised Ozzie's reporter antenna tone, which she used when sensing a story, as she asked, "Move backed here? From where?"

Kate laughed. "From many places, but I've finally been drawn back to the Cotswolds where I lived as a child. So what would you like from the kitchen?" Kate asked Ozzie, who gave her order.

Turning to Keya, Kate said, "I've spoken to Coll's sister, and she's already put you a jacket potato in the oven. She has some mushroom sauce left over. Will that be OK or would you prefer baked beans?"

"Oh, I'll try the mushroom sauce," enthused Keya. "It sounds different."

"And can we have another round of drinks?" asked Ozzie.

"Of course, I'll just hand your food order in first."

Kate left them as Ozzie asked, "Have you heard from Dotty?"

"Oh, I forgot." Keya reached into her coat pocket and removed a postcard. "This was waiting for me when I got home." She hadn't had a chance to read it properly but had been reassured that Dotty said she was well.

Keya placed the postcard with an image of a fountain on the table.

Ozzie picked it up and observed, "It's from Aix-en-Provence. Is that where she's living?"

"I think so. See what it says. I don't mind you reading it. I think she sent it for all of us."

Ozzie picked up the postcard and read.

"'Dear Keya, and everyone. Provence is amazing, just like the movies. Didier's mum knows all the best places to visit. This postcard is from Aix. We visited Cezanne's studio and an exhibition of his paintings. I'm well, and loving French food and cooking. So is Earl Grey. Love to all. Dotty.' She sounds very upbeat," added Ozzie, passing the postcard to Ryan.

"Someone on holiday?" asked Kate, as she placed their drinks on the table and thankfully handed Ozzie the bill.

"Our friend is taking a break," explained Keya. "She seems to be enjoying herself, but I miss her."

Kate looked down at the table as she said in a flat voice, "Friends are so important."

"Have you lost one?" asked Ozzie, her reporter antenna in action again.

Kate looked at her with a sad smile. "It was a long time ago." She glanced back as a customer approached the bar. "Excuse me."

"She's had a troubled past," remarked Ozzie.

"Well I like her," admitted Keya. "And even Coll, the landlord, is less grumpy when she's around. I need someone like her to run my cafe when I'm working."

Ryan reached for his pint and said, "Have you spoken to her about it?"

"Not yet, but perhaps I will. When the time is right," considered Keya.

"I wouldn't wait too long," advised Ozzie. "You never know what might happen."

CHAPTER FOUR

On Wednesday morning, Keya was driving one of her regular routes through the Cotswolds, showing a police presence and checking for fly-tipping and other misdemeanours. She pulled into a field entrance to let a large blue New Holland tractor pass.

The driver slowed to a stop and, pushing open the tractor's glass door, he climbed down the steps as Keya lowered her window. The farmer removed his baseball cap, which had the image of a fishing rod on it, and scratched his sandy hair.

"I'm sure we had thieves about again last night. Nothing's been taken, but it looks like someone's been trying to cut through the padlock on the barn where I keep the bailer and ploughs. I found scratch marks on it. And I heard old Mr Finch's quad bike is missing, again."

Keya groaned. Theft of farm equipment was on the rise in the area, and across the country. And she knew how much Mr Finch relied on his quad bike after his hip operation.

"Thanks for letting me know. I'll pop round and see him later. But what are you going to do?"

"Put up more spotlights. The farm already lights up like Cirencester marketplace whenever anyone drives in, and even foxes set the movement sensors off, but I think that's what spooked the thieves last night. That and me checking on a cow which is due to calve."

Keya thanked the farmer and waited for him to drive past, but before she eased off her hand brake, her phone buzzed. It was Gilly Wimsey from Akemans. She hoped the call wasn't to tell her Rowan and his team had been delayed again and hadn't arrived to dismantle the waterwheel.

"Hiya," said Keya, answering the call. "Has Rowan arrived?"

"Yes," replied Gilly in a strangled voice.

"What's wrong?" Keya asked sharply.

"You must come over, straight away. I don't want to say any more on the phone." Abruptly, Gilly ended the call. Gilly wasn't the calmest and most organised person, but she was usually upbeat, managing to juggle her various roles as a mother of two, wife to a doctor, and manager of the antiques centre. But something had clearly rattled her.

Keya resisted the temptation to speed round the country lanes, as she knew from experience that anything from a flock of sheep to Gilly's Lycra-clad husband on his bike could be round the next corner.

It took twenty-five minutes to reach Akemans. She parked in front of the antiques centre and hurried round to the back of the auction house.

"Oh toda!" she exclaimed as she collided with a man standing beside a vintage motorbike.

"Careful," admonished Brad, the elderly member of Vic's construction team.

"Sorry," she gushed as she reached down and helped him to his feet.

Carrying a smooth, round motorcycle helmet, Brad said, "You better come with me."

They found the other workmen gathered on the riverbank drinking tea and coffee and nibbling biscuits. Were those the chocolate chip cookies she'd brought yesterday?

Several of them looked behind them at the waterwheel as she approached and one called, "Gov."

Brad left as Gilly appeared, running her hand through her already dishevelled, orange curly hair.

She was accompanied by the site foreman, Vic Peters, who stopped beside the group of workmen and said, "All right, lads. Back to work. Tea break over."

Several of the men muttered and glanced across at the waterwheel as they shuffled into the old mill building.

When they'd left, Keya could see the waterwheel clearly, and the tall, willowy figure of Rowan Cartwright, wearing fluorescent orange trousers, standing on the stone wall separating the waterwheel channel from the river.

His team sat on the wall, against which two ladders had been secured, descending into the channel.

"Is there an issue with the waterwheel?" asked Keya as Gilly and Vic reached her.

Gilly's cheeks were flushed and, as she drew nearer, Keya noticed a sheen of sweat on her brow.

"Not the wheel itself," replied Vic in a strained voice.

"There's a body, Keya. A skeleton. Under the waterwheel." Gilly's voice rose in pitch and, instinctively, Keya stepped forward and placed a hand on her arm.

"What kind of skeleton?" Keya asked slowly, dreading the answer, but hoping it was an animal of some kind.

"A normal one, of course, although they only unearthed the top part. I think the rest is still hidden. Poor thing …" Gilly's voice trailed off.

Keya looked up at Vic, who was clutching his yellow hard hat under his arm.

"Rowan and his team were in the channel, removing some of the vegetation and earth which has built up at the bottom, so they could free the waterwheel. One of them found a sheet of plastic and when they pulled at it, it peeled back and revealed a human skull and bones. They clambered out of there pretty quick, I can tell you."

"I can't believe someone has been lying down there all these years," moaned Gilly.

It was time for Keya to take action, even though her body felt heavy. Who knew how long a police enquiry would go on and delay work on the waterwheel?

Gilly was clasping and unclasping her hands.

"Vic, can you give Gilly a cup of sweet tea?" asked Keya. "I'll call

Dr Peter and ask him to come over. Then I'll alert the police, unless you've already done it?"

Vic shook his head. "Gilly insisted we wait for you." He took Gilly's elbow and guided her towards the temporary entrance into the antiques centre while Keya reached for her phone.

"Hello, Keya," answered Dr Peter, Gilly's husband, in a jovial voice. "How is work progressing at Cotswold's most eagerly awaited cafe?"

"We've hit a snag." That was an understatement. She took a deep breath and continued, "A body, an old one I think, has been discovered beneath the waterwheel. Gilly's in shock and I wondered if you could come over?"

"That's terrible. What a gruesome discovery. I have one more patient I must see and then I'll be with you. Is someone with Gilly?"

"The foreman's taken her away and is hopefully giving her some sweet tea."

"What about George?" asked Dr Peter.

George, whose full name was George Carey-Boyd, was Gilly's intimidating sister who ran the auction house. Although she had been more civil since a recent trip to France, Keya was still scared of her.

"I'll contact her," assured Dr Peter. "I'm sure you've enough to deal with."

Which was true, but she was still grateful to Dr Peter. Her next call was to her boss, Inspector Evans.

He answered with a gruff, "Sergeant, trouble on the farm?"

"No, sir. At the mill, or should I say at Akemans."

Keya heard him sigh. Over the past eighteen months there had been quite a lot of trouble at Akemans, including a murder during an auction.

His deep baritone Welsh voice said, "How bad is it?"

"I'm not sure yet. The scene isn't easily accessible, but the site foreman told me they've found a skeleton."

"So not a recent death then?"

"Not unless …' Keya stopped. She didn't want her mind going down the route of gruesome deaths. Instead, she explained, "It was found buried under plastic, earth and vegetation."

"Very well. You know the drill. Constable Jenkins and I will join you shortly. I sent Sergeant Unwin to Gloucester for a regional meeting. He's better at politics than me. I presume we'll need SOCOs for this one?"

SOCOs were scenes of crime officers. Gloucestershire Police used a civilian company in Cheltenham on a consultancy basis.

"I expect so, sir."

"I'll contact them, but I've no idea how long they'll take. Can you cover the body to protect it?"

"I'll see what I can do."

"Sorry business, Sergeant," Inspector Evans remarked as he ended the call.

CHAPTER FIVE

When Keya had finished her call to Inspector Evans, she turned back towards the river. Makeshift steps had been created down to the riverbank and the stone bridge which Gilly had so fondly told her she'd jumped off as a child on summer days.

The bridge had been widened with wooden planks for access to the far stone wall and had a metal scaffolding-pole handrail.

Brad was standing at the bottom of the makeshift steps staring at the waterwheel.

Keya stopped at the top of the steps and waited until she had the attention of Rowan and his team.

"This is now a crime scene," she shouted. "Please make your way back to the bank, being careful not to disturb anything."

Lazily, the four men, including the exceptionally tall Rowan, and one woman, stepped up onto the dividing wall and followed each other in single file back across the bridge and up the makeshift steps.

When they'd gathered in a group in front of Keya, she announced, "Myself or my colleagues will speak to each of you in turn, but for now I need to protect the crime scene. Is it definitely a human skeleton you found?"

In response, one of the team, who Keya now realised was a woman with a shaved head, removed her phone and said, "I took some photos, in case you asked. I'm also an archaeologist, so I'm used to working with old bones."

Keya took the phone and stared at the image of a skull, neck bones, and part of the ribs. Zooming in, she realised there was a hole in the skull, above the left eye socket, and fractures running across the top of it. Caused before or after death, she wondered.

The woman said, "I'd say the skull is female, as the head is thinner and the chin more pointed than a male one, and it's smaller, so in my opinion an older child or young adolescent."

Keya's eyes widened. "Wow, that's really useful. I don't suppose you know how long it's been down there?"

"At least twenty years, if not more, from the grass and wild campion that has established itself."

Rowan, whose voice Keya thought surprisingly high-pitched for a man approaching seven feet tall, said, "Won't there be police record if a child went missing? Surely someone would have been looking for them."

'I'm sure there is, and Constable Jenkins or I will be tasked with looking back through all the missing person reports." It was not a job she relished.

"And now, Rowan, can you and your colleagues find somewhere to wait until my boss arrives?"

Chattering amongst themselves, Rowan's team entered the old mill building.

Keya called down to Brad and asked, "Brad, can you wait here for me and make sure nobody accesses the crime scene?"

Brad didn't respond.

"Brad, did you hear me?" called Keya again.

He looked up at her with a blank expression and replied softly, so she only just caught his words, "Och, I'll do that."

Keya returned to her car in front of the antiques centre and was just removing a reel of blue tape with the repeated words 'POLICE - INCIDENT SCENE - KEEP OUT' printed on it when a squad car pulled up beside her.

As Inspector Evans climbed out, wearing his habitual brown suit, he declared, "I wasn't expecting to return to Akemans so soon. Dotty Sayers had a habit of poking her nose in where it didn't belong and discovering dead bodies, and I hope you haven't caught her bug, Sergeant."

He eyed her grimly before asking, "Where is the body?"

"At the back of what was the old mill, next to the river, beneath the waterwheel."

"That sounds tricky." The inspector had the stocky look of an ex-rugby player, which he was, and the red, chubby cheeks of someone who enjoyed a pint or two of beer.

Just then there was the tinkle of a bicycle bell and Dr Peter Wimsey, Gilly's husband, wearing Lycra cycling leggings and a bright yellow jacket, braked to a stop. Ryan, who had climbed out of the driver's side of the squad car, stepped to one side.

"Doctor," grunted Inspector Evans. "I think it's too late for your services."

Dr Peter removed his cycling helmet and said, "I've come to see Gilly. How is she doing?" He directed his question at Keya.

"I'm not sure. Vic took her inside while I sorted out the crime scene."

"I'll go and find her." Dr Peter pushed his bike towards the entrance to the antiques centre.

"Go with him, Constable, and start taking statements," directed Inspector Evans.

Keya watched Ryan's tall figure catch up with Dr Peter before turning back to her car and picking up the crime scene tape again.

"Let's get on with it," instructed the inspector and he and Keya returned to the riverbank.

"Where is it?" asked the inspector, standing at the top of the temporary steps, looking towards the water wheel.

"I don't think it's visible from here. The team that found it climbed down those ladders into what used to be a channel funnelling river water to the waterwheel to power the mill."

"And how do you get over there?" The inspector rocked on his heels and looked dubiously towards the ladders.

"Down the steps and across the stone bridge," replied Keya.

"I think I'll wait for the SOCO, but you start by taping off the access to the bridge."

Keya descended the makeshift steps, holding onto the handrail as they were slippery.

"I need to tape off across to the bridge," she told Brad. "Where do you suggest I tie it?"

"There's an old drainpipe, running down the wall of the flour mill. The bottom's rusted off, but it should be sturdy enough," he replied.

Keya handed Brad the free end of the roll of tape, which she unravelled as he walked towards the old mill building until there was enough to tie it to the drainpipe.

"What about the other end?" she asked when Brad returned.

"How about that fence post?" Brad pointed towards a wooden stake protruding from the riverbank a few metres away.

"That should work. Can you do it?" The stake was precariously close to the edge of the river and Keya didn't want to trip and fall into the water.

Brad was still tying the tape when Keya heard a man greet Inspector Evans.

His voice was matter of fact and businesslike as he said, "Inspector, I understand you've found a body and need our help." He wore a white all-in-one protective suit, although the hood hung down the back of his neck.

A similarly clad younger colleague stood at the far side of a walkway of wooden planks, spanning a patch of bare earth, contemplating how to pull a large aluminium box on wheels over the planks.

"So I believe. But I've not seen it myself. It's over there." Inspector Evans pointed towards the bottom of the ladders.

"Graham, leave that for now. Let's see what we have first," instructed the senior SOCO.

Graham's shoulders sagged as he pushed the extending handle back down into the aluminium box and crossed the planks.

Both SOCOs ducked under the crime scene tape and climbed onto the stone bridge. The senior one stopped and turned round. "One of you needs to come with us," he stated.

"You go, Sergeant. But BE careful," directed Inspector Evans.

Keya took a deep breath. She knew why the inspector was warning her. She had a habit of being clumsy and this time it would be her, or one of the SOCOs, in the river or down in the channel if she tripped.

Gingerly, she approached the low stone bridge and realised a series of shallow steps was carved into it. Clasping the protruding scaffolding-pole handrail, she pulled herself up and onto the bridge.

Despite the extra width provided by the wooden planks, she still stepped slowly across, placing one foot cautiously in front of the other, like a gymnast performing on the beam.

The pair of SOCOs were already on the stone wall, looking back at her impatiently. The wall was even narrower than the bridge, and she shuffled along sideways, holding her arms out for balance, until she reached the first ladder.

"Stay here for now," instructed the senior SOCO. "We don't want you trampling around the crime scene."

Charming, thought Keya. Was she just expected to wobble about on top of the wall? She contemplated siting down but thought getting back up would be more of a challenge.

The two SOCOs were surprisingly agile, and soon descended the ladders and pulled their hoods over their heads.

"Whose footprints are these?" the senior one asked.

"Members of the team who were dismantling and removing the waterwheel," Keya replied, leaning forward.

The SOCOs tried to step around the footprints but soon gave up as the channel was less than a metre wide and the ground uneven. Most of an old, partly disintegrated, white plastic sack was visible. The company name was worn away, but Keya could still read the word 'fertiliser'.

Growing nearby were the white trumpet-shaped flowers of the calla lily. She knew they represented death, but also resurrection and life.

Under the direction of the senior SOCO, Graham, the younger colleague, lifted up the end of the plastic bag to reveal a dirty white skull and the top section of a human skeleton.

"I'm not sure if this is the cause of death," the senior SOCO pointed to the hole in the skull, "but someone gave her a nasty bang."

"So it is a woman?" called down Keya as she leaned closer to the SOCOs.

"No, too small. I'd say a girl of between ten and twelve years."

Poor thing, thought Keya. "Any idea how long she's been down there?"

"Hard to say," called back the SOCO, "but I think they stopped using these types of sacks twenty years ago, so at least that."

This was not her usual case. A twenty-year-old body of a young girl.

She straightened up, but too quickly. She wobbled. Leaning back, so as not to fall into the channel, a stone in the wall rocked under her foot.

"Oh toda!" she cried as she fell backwards into the river.

CHAPTER SIX

Keya sat in the builders' breakout area next to Vic Peters' office. It was actually part of the old mill which had been incorporated into the antiques centre but had now been stripped out ready to be turned into the cafe.

There were benches and trestle tables, and on one table, a water heater which provided constant boiling water for 'brews', as the builders termed their teas and coffees, and for rehydrating pots of noodles, rice and soup for lunches and snacks.

A combination of smells including mushroom, tomato, and Chinese spices lingered in the air, and Keya tried not to taste them as she sipped her tea. She was sitting on a bench away from the main breakout area, wrapped in a blanket. After her ungainly tumble into the River Coln, she'd been swept across to the far bank where she'd managed to grab hold of a protruding tree root and pull herself half out of the chilling water.

After resting on the bank, her legs still immersed in the river, she'd been contemplating how to continue her progress through the thick undergrowth when she heard Ryan shout, "Keya, where are you?"

"Over here," she'd called back.

A sound of breaking branches followed, and Ryan had appeared with two of the builders and hauled her to safety. She'd bowed her head as she'd made soggy progress back to Akemans via the main bridge over the River Coln.

Luckily, her keys, wallet and phone were in a zipped pocket, as she'd already lost each of them on more than one occasion. Ryan had been able to fetch spare clothes from her car but they were a strange mixture of sports leggings and a t-shirt which she was now wearing with black rubber wellies and a high-vis jacket.

She'd been most grateful to Gilly Wimsey, who'd lent her a towel and chaperoned her to Akemans' shower, as she left a watery trail across the antiques centre floor. Gilly had seemed relieved to be busy and fussed about asking if there was anything else she needed. They avoided any talk about skeletons.

Keya's hair was wet from the shower and her legs still felt the chill of river water but the large space heater near her, which the builders were using to dry plaster on the new wall separating the cafe from the antiques centre, offered some welcome warmth as did her tea.

"Let's have a look at you," said Dr Peter in a matter-of-fact voice as he leaned towards her. "Any dizziness or nausea? Any painful areas from bangs or knocks?"

"No, but I'm still waiting for all the feeling to return to my legs, and my hands and face are itchy."

"That's not a surprise. You have quite a few scratches, I presume from where you climbed out onto the riverbank. You were lucky not to hit your head on the wall as you fell."

"I wonder if that's what happened to the girl?"

"Which girl?" asked Dr Peter, wrinkling his nose.

"The one we've found at the bottom of the waterwheel channel."

"But Gilly said it was a skeleton."

"It is, but the senior SOCO said it was female, but too small for a fully grown woman. Do you know of any girls who've gone missing around here?"

"Not since I've lived in the area, but that's only been fifteen years. Is the skeleton younger or older than that?"

"Probably older."

"Then it won't be an easy job discovering who it is."

"I know," groaned Keya, envisaging the mountains of paperwork she'd be wading through this afternoon. And if the body was over twenty-five years old, she'd have to start looking through paper records, as not all police officers had used digital ones in the early 1990s.

She glanced across at Ryan who was talking to one of Rowan's team.

He stood up and, joining her and Dr Peter, said, "I'm finished interviewing the waterwheel renovation team, although there wasn't much they could tell me. As soon as they discovered the skeleton, they climbed out of the channel and waited for you to arrive."

He glanced down at Keya's wellies. "Shall I ask the inspector if I can drive you home before going to the station, so you can change into something more comfortable?"

"I'll come with you to speak to him," replied Keya, standing up. She handed her half-drunk cup of tea to Ryan and picked up the blanket. "Can you give this to Gilly," she asked Dr Peter as she handed it to him, "and say thanks."

"Of course, and I think I'll tell her to go home, too, on doctor's orders. She's had a nasty shock." Dr Peter carefully folded the blanket.

As Keya and Ryan walked out of the old mill, Ryan asked, "Why did Gilly have a nasty shock? There's been trouble at Akemans before, hasn't there?"

"Too true," agreed Keya, "and usually involving Dotty." But her smile faded when she thought of another young woman who'd been murdered during an auction. Everyone had been upset, but not with the depth of emotion Gilly was now showing.

"Actually, that's a really good point. I think I need to speak to Gilly again. I'll drive myself home, carefully," she glanced down at her wellies, "and after I've changed, visit Gilly at home, where she might feel more comfortable speaking to me."

Dressed in her spare uniform, and with her hair dried and tied back in a bun, Keya drove to Coln Akeman and parked in front of Gilly and Dr Peter Wimsey's double-fronted Cotswold stone house.

Lights were on in the room to the right of the front door, which she knew was the waiting room for Dr Peter's surgery. She walked round to the side door of the house and pressed the bell.

Although she heard its ding-dong sound inside, nobody answered the door. She tried again, but still no response.

Standing back, she looked to her left. There was a light on in the kitchen. She pushed the bell for a third time.

"All right, all right, I'm coming," called Gilly's strained voice. She opened the door to Keya and gasped. In a small voice, she asked, "Do you know who it is? The skeleton."

Keya considered Gilly, with her bloodshot eyes and the snot running from her nose, which she mopped up with the tissue in her hand.

With a glimmer of understanding, Keya replied gently, "No. But I think you do?"

Gilly leaned back as she clamped her lips together and stared at Keya. Then she opened her mouth and let out a deep breath. "You better come in."

Gilly didn't lead her to the chaotic kitchen, where Keya had sat the few times she'd visited with Dotty, but instead, they walked into the dining room. There was a photograph album open on the mahogany dining table.

"May I?" Keya asked.

Gilly nodded.

The album was open at a page which mostly showed photos of three girls, aged somewhere between ten and twelve, in swimming costumes in or beside the river at Akemans. The photos had a brown sepia tint, which gave them a nostalgic look.

"Is this you, George and a friend?" Keya asked, pointing to the three girls standing on the water channel bridge. They looked cold despite the blue sky.

"George didn't join us, not then. She was too high and mighty to be messing around in the river, although she still played with me that year at the beach at Weymouth. We used to stay in the same bed and breakfast each summer for two weeks with Mum, and my dad joined us at weekends, although he always turned his nose up at our accommodation and argued with Mum that we could afford a hotel."

Gilly laughed. "But my mum told him he was a snob and she preferred to help the local economy rather than put money in the pockets of a hotel chain. But I digress." Gilly's attention returned to the open photo album, and she placed a finger next to the photo of the three girls. "That's me, the summer after I left primary school with my two best friends, Rachael and Katherine."

Gilly's eyes took in other photos of the girls swimming, or sunbathing on the riverbank, or eating a picnic.

"Is that Aunt Beanie?" gasped Keya, pointing to a woman with a blue shirt with the collar turned up.

Gilly laughed again. "Yes, and look at her hair. I think she must have permed it."

Aunt Beanie's hair was honey-blonde back then and huge in volume with curls which reached to her neck.

"I remember it was so hot in July that we swam most days, and Aunt Beanie would bring us a picnic, or ice creams, or cold drinks. We had such fun ..." Gilly's voice trailed off as she fiddled with the corner of the page.

The photograph nearest Gilly's hand was blurred but showed a larger group of boys and girls, dressed in shorts and t-shirts, and Keya thought she recognised George, as well as Gilly's two friends.

"Who's in this photo?" she asked.

Gilly sniffed. "I took that photo. It was the day before Mum took us to the beach. George and her friend Nathan, Rachael's brother, and his friends joined us by the river in the afternoon. I think some of them brought beers and cider and we had a small party. It was such fun."

Gilly's sniffs turned to sobs, and she turned away from Keya.

Quietly, Keya asked, "But something happened, didn't it?"

Gilly nodded her head, but she remained with her back to Keya.

Keya waited, sensing that whatever Gilly had to tell her was important, but understanding it must be difficult returning to her past.

For several minutes, all she heard were sobs until Gilly's shoulders heaved and she turned to face Keya.

"That was the last time I saw Rachael and Katherine. When we returned from the seaside, they were both gone."

"Gone?" gasped Keya.

"Katherine and her father moved to Scotland. He had a new job there. And Rachael ..." Gilly paused and took a deep, ragged breath. "Nobody knew where she was. I think it's her body under the waterwheel."

CHAPTER SEVEN

"I'm so sorry. It must be a real shock to find your friend's body. But what did you think had happened to her at the time?" asked Keya, gently.

Gilly sat back and stared over Keya's shoulder with a faraway look. "Rachael was the oldest of us. I think she was kept back a year at school because she'd been ill. Meningitis or scarlet fever, or something like that. And she was more mature, probably because she had an older brother, Nathan.

She sometimes wore make-up although I heard her mum shouting at her in her Welsh accent one day when she'd found Rachael had borrowed her lipstick."

Gilly smiled at the recollection.

"And I know Katherine's dad didn't approve of her as a friend for his daughter. He was a single parent. The rumour was that his wife, Katherine's mother, had run away to Germany with a soldier. I've no idea if that was true or not. But he was rather overprotective of Katherine and didn't like it when Rachael's brother and his friends were around."

"Like in the photo?" asked Keya.

"Yes. That's right." Gilly paused.

Slowly she said, as if dragging the memory from her brain, "Mr

Dewsbury, Katherine's dad, was furious when he found us by the river. I think I said that Nathan and his friends had been drinking. Well one of them, I can't remember who, confronted Mr Dewsbury and got punched in the face for his troubles. There was blood everywhere. It must have been a broken nose."

Gilly wiped her own nose.

"Aunt Beanie came storming round the corner of the auction house and tore a strip off Mr Dewsbury. He did some work for Akemans, just odd jobs and gardening and that sort of thing, so I don't think he dared fight back. I'm not sure what happened after that. I think one of the older boys, who could drive, took his friend to hospital."

A single tear appeared in the corner of Gilly's eye. "Aunt Beanie took me inside and said it was time to go home. I remember looking back at Katherine, who had become the focus of her father's anger while Rachael tried to reason with him, until Nathan dragged her away too."

Gilly half-laughed. "The last image I have of Rachael is sticking Vs up at Mr Dewsbury, and Katherine smiling behind her father's back."

Gilly stopped speaking and Keya gave her a few minutes of contemplation before she asked, "Do you think Mr Dewsbury could have killed Rachael?"

"What? He was overprotective of his own daughter, so he was hardly likely to harm someone else's. Besides, he and Katherine moved to Scotland. I've no idea if he was even around when Rachael disappeared. Probably more likely to be one of those salesman or contract workers who stayed at the pub. Rachael's parents owned the Axeman which also offered bed and breakfast back then.

"It had three single rooms with a shared bathroom, and one larger ensuite room. I remember helping Rachel clean them one Saturday and getting paid £20. But I'm sure the police interviewed all the guests, and nobody was arrested. I left for boarding school that autumn and had my own troubles, and I didn't hear much more about Rachael's disappearance."

Again, Gilly paused, as if trying to recall the past. "Rachael's dad died, just before Christmas I think, the following year, and I heard her mother moved back to Wales, to her family. Nathan wasn't interested in running the pub, so he sold it and I've no idea where he went."

She looked up at Keya. "And that's all I remember about it. I didn't even go to Rachael's memorial service, a year after her disappearance, as I was away with Mum."

Keya checked her black-strapped watch. "I need to get back to the police station. Will you be OK on your own?"

"What time is it?" asked Gilly.

"Three fifteen."

"The kids will be home from school soon and they're bound to be hungry." Gilly took a final look at the photograph album before closing it.

"Do you mind if I take that?" asked Keya.

Gilly hesitated.

"I won't submit it as evidence. If we need any of the photos, I'll photocopy or scan them and return the originals to you."

"OK." Gilly pushed the album across to Keya.

The front cover was a faded green colour and when Keya picked it up, she realised it was padded.

"But promise me you'll look after it?" Gilly insisted.

"I will."

It was nearly four o'clock by the time Keya had driven to Cirencester, found an alternative parking space, as a small red Toyota was parked in her allocated space, and entered the police station. She found Ryan in their team room and heard Inspector Evans on the phone.

"How difficult can it be?" shouted the inspector.

Keya sat down at her desk, opposite Ryan's, and next to Sergeant Unwin's unoccupied place as Inspector Evans stalked out of his office. "Can anyone show me where the files are from 1989?" he demanded.

"There are only a few on the system, sir," replied Ryan.

The archives clerk, the recently retired Sergeant Rowbottom, carried two cardboard document boxes into the room and dumped them beside the others, piled up beside Ryan's desk.

"If I'm not busy once I've finished delivering all your boxes, I'll help you go through them," Sergeant Rowbottom offered. "I probably remember most of the cases."

"Thanks, Sergeant," replied Ryan. "That would be really helpful."

"No bother and, remember, it's Stan now."

Neither Keya, or Ryan it seemed, had got used to Sergeant Rowbottom, Stan's, retirement. It had happened quickly when he'd volunteered for redundancy during the cutbacks the previous month, saying he was fed up with dealing with drunken idiots on a Friday night.

"What's all this?" asked Inspector Evans belligerently, pointing to all the boxes.

"The missing person and case files young Ryan asked for," replied Stan, ignoring the Inspector's hostile tone.

"Haven't they been digitised?"

"No. The programme was cut. Lack of funding."

Inspector Evans rolled his eyes. "This is going to take forever. How are we going to find out who the dead girl is when ..."

"Actually," interrupted Keya, "I think I might know."

"Then why didn't you say so?" the inspector blustered, turning his frustration on Keya.

"Sorry," she apologised, not bothering to add that she hadn't yet had the opportunity to speak.

"Well go on. Don't keep us in suspense," insisted Inspector Evans.

Keya stood and picked up the photograph album she'd brought from Gilly's house. As she opened it on Ryan's desk, the inspector demanded in an exasperated tone, "Why are we looking at holiday snaps of the seaside?"

"Just a minute, sir." She found the right page and pointed to Gilly's friend, Rachael. "This girl went missing the summer Gilly Wimsey left primary school."

"Is that the lass that disappeared from The Axeman in Coln Akeman?" asked Stan. He inhaled and shook his head. "Bad business that. We were certain it was one of the men staying at the pub, but they all had alibis. But that must be going back thirty years or more."

"Before my time," conceded Inspector Evans, his face returning to its normal colour as he calmed down. "Do you remember what she was called?"

"Fawcett was the family name," recalled Stan.

"Rachael," added Keya.

"That's right, the missing lass was Rachael Fawcett," stated Stan.

Ryan tapped away on his computer until he stopped and read, "Rachael Emily Fawcett, aged 12, was last seen riding her bike through Coln Akeman on Thursday 3rd August 1989."

"Rightio," responded Stan. "Let me fetch the relevant box." He picked up the two he'd just brought and left the room.

"What else does it say on your computer?" Inspector Evans asked Ryan.

"Not much. The case is unsolved, and the victim presumed dead. It gives a case file and document number."

Stan returned with another box. "Here we are, 'Serious Crimes, July to September 1989'."

CHAPTER EIGHT

Stan removed the lid of the cardboard document box with a flourish, like a magician revealing a rabbit.

Inside there was a row of green file holders, and inside most of them a single sheet of paper. Ryan picked one out and read, "Murder of Dennis Matthews. See digital records. And then it gives a case number."

Stan sucked in a breath. "That was a nasty one. A brawl in the street after an argument about money in a pub in Stroud. He was killed with a broken bottle and, despite there being at least thirty people in the street, they all denied seeing anything. It wasn't until two young women admitted that they'd been threatened and told not to tell us what they'd seen, that we caught the culprit. I think he's up for parole next month."

"This is the one we want," enthused Ryan, breaking into Stan's reminiscence. He pulled out a grey folder, thick with papers, and then a second one, equally well stuffed.

"That should keep you busy for the rest of the day," observed Inspector Evans. "I've a meeting with our new Assistant Chief Constable to give him an update on the case. At least I can tell him we have a potential name, subject to DNA confirmation. I presume we do have the victim's DNA on file?"

"I'm not sure," replied Ryan.

"We should have," confirmed Stan. "It was standard procedure from 1985."

Inspector Evans left the room as Keya asked, "How do you think we should tackle this? Just reading through the files doesn't feel very efficient."

"Agreed," said Ryan. "Why don't I set up a dummy electronic file and we'll start as we would any investigation today? We'll read the documents and you tell me anything of importance, and I'll add it into our new case file."

"OK," Keya agreed, picking up the top file and taking it to her desk.

"Shall I sit at Sergeant Onion's desk?" asked Stan, entering the room.

There were many members of Cirencester police station who'd latched onto Inspector Evans' derisory nickname for Sergeant Unwin, as they begrudged the young sergeant his good looks, fast-track progress and ambitious nature.

It didn't help that he'd been Chief Inspector Ringrose's golden boy and had acted rather pompously until the chief inspector's enforced retirement.

He'd also arrested Keya's friend Dotty, for which she hadn't entirely forgiven him.

"Yes," replied Ryan. "I doubt he'll be back. There's a drinks reception after his conference today."

"That'll be right up his street," muttered Stan. "Hobnobbing with the top brass and local dignitaries."

Keya decided to make her own notes, rather than disturb Ryan with each individual piece of information.

Silence had just descended on the room when Ryan's phone rang.

"Uh-oh!" He answered the call. "Hi, Ozzie."

Keya stared at Ryan, who looked uneasy as he shuffled in his chair.

"You know, I can't comment until we've formally identified the body." He listened and then said, "She has, has she? Well I can't confirm or deny that." Another pause. "No, I'm not being difficult, but this is an old case and a sensitive one, as it involves a young girl."

Oops, thought Keya.

Flushing Ryan said, "No, I've already said too much. You'll have to call the press office." He ended the call and breathed deeply. "Ozzie's not going to let this one go. I've no idea why, but she spoke to Aunt Beanie, who told her about Rachael's disappearance."

"Should we let the inspector know?" suggested Keya.

"I would," agreed Stan.

"I'll send him a message." Keya tapped the keys on her phone before placing it in her pocket and returning to the papers in the file.

She discovered that Gilly was right, and that Rachael's mother had been Welsh, and she'd returned to her family after her husband's death. Nathan Fawcett, Rachael's brother, had sold the pub and moved to Australia. She wondered if he was still there.

She was making a note to check when a death certificate caught her eye. Stapled to it was a handwritten memo which she presumed had been added sometime after Rachael's disappearance.

Keya scanned the memo and then said, "This is interesting. Seven years after Rachael disappeared, her brother, Nathan, applied for her to be declared legally dead. The courts agreed and, according to whoever wrote this - I can't read the signature - Nathan collected the outstanding funds from the sale of The Axeman, which had been set aside for Rachael."

So it seemed Nathan had returned from Australia. She crossed out her note.

"How much?" asked Ryan.

"The pub sold for £300,000."

"That was worth a lot back then," disclosed Stan. "You could buy a decent sized house and still have change in your pocket. But The Axeman was a popular pub."

"I wonder if that's what Nathan did? Buy a house." Keya logged into her computer and searched for the name Nathan Fawcett. There were several entries on the system for tax infringements.

She found the last address he'd given and checked it against the electoral roll. He was no longer the occupant, but a wider search of the database provided a new address.

"I think I've found him. He moved into a house on The Paddock, Siddington, three years ago."

Stan whistled. "Something went right for him. That's the new estate they've built. And it's very exclusive … and expensive."

"Here's the list of men staying at The Axeman the week Rachael went missing," said Ryan, pulling out a sheet of paper. "Two of them were construction workers, building industrial units on the edge of Swindon, one of them is listed as a motor salesman, and the fifth just says businessman, but someone added a note that he was house-hunting in the area."

Keya's phone jingled in her pocket. She pulled it out, glanced at the caller ID and groaned. "Hi, Zivah. I'm sorry. We've got a new case."

"There's always something. What is it this time?" her younger sister retorted.

"A skeleton of a young girl."

"A skeleton. Then it's hardly going to matter if you leave work early today … or even when you're supposed to." Zivah sounded indignant, but Keya had become used to her sister's tone and the fact that she thought her upcoming marriage the most important event of the year.

"So are you coming?" Zivah demanded.

"Where? Oh toda! Yes, I'm just leaving." Keya ended the call, cutting off her sister's verbal onslaught.

"What was that about?" asked Stan.

"I'm supposed to be at a dress fitting for my sister's wedding. And she's not happy that I've forgotten."

"She didn't sound it," chuckled Stan.

"I better go," said Keya, standing up. "I'll finish going through this tomorrow." She handed Ryan the notes she'd jotted down. "Sorry to bail on you."

"That's OK," Ryan smiled back. "You must be very excited about the wedding."

"Not really," sighed Keya. "But at least we've persuaded pa not to extend it to five days. Three is quite enough."

"Three days?" Ryan's eyes widened.

"Yes. Three days for me to endure the barbed comments of my relatives, as I'm not the one getting married. And I'm the oldest."

Stan chuckled again. "Take young Ryan with you. That'll get them talking."

Keya's eyes twinkled as she regarded Ryan. "I might just do that."

CHAPTER NINE

Keya drove to Cheltenham along the A417, concentrating hard on not exceeding the speed limit which was so easy to do in her super-charged Ford Focus, given to her by the traffic division.

She was proud of her car but didn't think her sister would appreciate her parking it outside Laboni's dress shop. It was very conspicuous with distinctive blue and yellow squares on its sides, and a strip of blue and white lights across its roof.

It was after five o'clock so Keya thought it would be OK to park in a residential street just off the main A40 which ran though Montpellier, an area of Cheltenham with boutique dress shops and upmarket restaurants and wine bars.

She walked back to the A40 and hurried along the pavement before turning into another side street, passing a cafe, and entering Laboni's.

Three faces turned towards her.

"At last, Keya. I thought you were never coming." Zivah was sitting in a gold upholstered chair with their youngest sister, Maitri, beside her perched on the arm. Standing protectively on the other side was Zivah's best friend, Ira.

Zivah had an album with sketches and photographs of henna body art, known as mehandi, open on her lap.

"Here are some more modern examples which you might prefer," announced the assistant as she walked towards them from the back of the shop. She looked up and nearly dropped the portfolio she was carrying. She stammered, "Is there a problem, officer?"

"The only problem is that my sister is late," declared Zivah.

The shop assistant raised her eyebrows. "You're Keya?"

Keya nodded.

Suddenly businesslike, the shop assistant handed the portfolio she was carrying to Ira and beckoned to Keya. "Follow me."

At the rear of the shop, there was a dressing rail outside two curtained-off changing booths, holding a collection of embroidered lehangas, the skirt and top combinations in wonderful pastel shades.

Keya was expecting vivid traditional wedding colours of orange and red.

"Your sister said no trousers. But these pastel shades are all the rage amongst Bollywood actresses. You're a size 10?"

"Yes," replied Keya hypnotised by the stunning outfits. "Wow, I don't know where to start. Does Zivah have any favourites?"

The shop assistant removed a pale turquoise-blue jacket with delicate organza half sleeves. It was short and fitted, with elegant gold embroidery around the collar and hem.

"That's gorgeous!" exclaimed Keya.

"And one of these skirts to go with it?" The shop assistant held up two floating, floor-length skirts of the same pale turquoise. One was heavily embroidered all over and the other only around the hem. The second one also had ribbons and ruffles around the bottom.

"Can I try that one?" asked Keya, pointing to the second skirt.

Using one of the curtained changing booths, she pulled off her impersonal black and white uniform and slipped on the fitted jacket, fastening the small silk buttons. If she wore this outfit, she'd need to wear a cami top beneath it. Stepping into the skirt she pulled it up and fastened the back. She smoothed her jacket over her shirt, took a deep breath, and left the changing room.

"Keya, let's have a look!" called her sister.

Barefooted, Keya tiptoed to the front of the shop and stood self-consciously in front of her sisters and Ira, none of whom had moved since she'd left them. The shop assistant approached and undid Keya's bun so her dark brown hair fell to her shoulders.

"Wow, sis, you look beautiful," gasped Zivah.

"Her police uniform certainly doesn't do her any favours," agreed the shop assistant.

Maitri giggled.

Ira didn't join in the adulation but stood with her lips pressed together. Ira's waist had thickened over the last couple of years. Was she jealous of Keya's figure? Keya chuckled to herself as Ira jabbed Zivah in the shoulder.

"Go on, tell her," whispered Ira, insistently.

Zivah's face softened as she considered her older sister. "Keya, you look beautiful and will surely find a husband at the wedding."

Keya's shoulders slumped, and she exhaled noisily.

"But I know how busy you are, and I need someone who has the time and … commitment, to help me prepare for the wedding, and I don't think that's you."

True enough, thought Keya to herself.

Zivah continued, "So Ira asked if she could perform the sisterly duties?"

"What about me?" cried Maitri.

"You've exams to study for," dismissed Zivah.

"Do you mind?" asked Zivah, staring at Keya with pleading eyes.

"Mind? Why should I? Sorry, sis, it's not that I don't want to be there and support you on your big day, but weddings are not really my thing."

Zivah smiled slowly in relief. "That's what I thought," and she held her hands out towards Keya.

Keya stepped forward and clasped them as she said, "You do what you think best. It's your big day." And she kissed her sister on the cheek.

As she straightened up, she noted Ira's pinched expression. It was all or nothing, she considered. If Ira was to step into her duties as the older sister, she'd have to accept that she would be sidelined.

She looked over at the fresh, radiant face of Maitri. But at least that meant she could have fun. Perhaps she would invite Ryan after all. What would her relatives make of him? A young, blonde-haired white man, well in excess of six feet, who could talk about sport, business and tech matters with ease. The perfect partner.

It was half past eight by the time Keya arrived back at Ampney St Martin. Instead of going home to change, she parked outside the Dog and Duck and entered the pub.

"Evening, Sergeant," called Derek, her landlord, from his seat by the window. One of his village mates, Bernard, was sitting next to him on the bench, their half-drunk pints of beer on the table in front of them.

"Hiya, Derek," she replied as she strode across to the bar.

"What can I get you?" asked Kate.

"Is Coll still away?" responded Keya.

"He won't be back until next week. But it's quiet in here at the moment. Were you wanting food? It's just that Coll's sister left early, as there were no customers eating this evening."

Keya's stomach gurgled in answer.

Kate smiled. "Let me see what I can find."

"And can I have a cup of tea?"

"I'll put the kettle on."

Kate disappeared around the back of the bar as Derek called over, "I hear there's activity at Akemans."

"What sort of activity, Derek?" asked Keya as she walked across to his table and stopped opposite him and Bernard, who grinned at her, toothlessly.

"The sort that involves forensic specialists wearing white suits."

"And how do you know about that?"

"It was on the TV. Someone filmed it on their phone."

Of course they did, thought Keya. That's the trouble these days. Nothing is secret if someone is around with a phone. But who had filmed the SOCOs? Brad?

Bernard nudged Derek with his elbow, and Derek glanced at him before asking, "Did you enjoy your swim?"

Keya groaned. Someone had also filmed her falling off the wall.

"What are you two cackling about?" asked Kate as she returned, carrying Keya's tea. "Where would you like to sit?"

"We were asking the sergeant if she enjoyed her swim in the river today. We watched her tumble off a wall at the back of Akemans, where they've discovered a skeleton." Derek smirked at Bernard.

Keya began, "Derek ..."

But there was a smashing of crockery behind her.

"How clumsy of me!" Kate cried.

"What's got into her?" asked Bernard, wrinkling his already lined forehead.

Keya frowned at Derek and Bernard before turning to Kate and sympathising, "That's my speciality, dropping things. Can I help tidy up?" she asked as she noticed Kate's grey pallor.

"I'll grab the dustpan and brush, and the mop." Kate fetched a light-green dustpan and brush, which she silently handed to Keya.

As Keya collected broken ceramic pieces of cup and saucer, she heard Derek say, "I remember a lassie going missing one summer at Coln Akeman. From the pub. Did they ever find her?"

Bernard pushed his toothless gums together and shook his head. "Not that I recall, but it was a long time ago."

Derek watched Keya. "Before you were born, Sergeant."

"I'm not sure about that," Keya replied as Kate reappeared, carrying a red plastic bucket and sponge-ended mop. "I am thirty-three."

"You look twenty-five to me," remarked Derek innocently.

Keya stared at him, and Bernard burst out laughing but soon bent over, consumed with dry racking coughs.

"Careful there, drink your pint," advised Derek.

When the teacup and its contents had been cleared away, Keya returned to the bar and Kate joined her, carrying a fresh cup of tea and a bowl of bubbling macaroni cheese accompanied by two large slices of garlic bread.

"Perfect, thanks," said Keya, as she pulled herself up onto a tall bar stool.

"Do you mind if I have a drink?" asked Kate.

"Help yourself," spluttered Keya as she fanned her mouth. The macaroni cheese was certainly hot. "But are you driving home?"

Kate pressed a glass up to a black tap attached to a large, upturned bottle of vodka, mounted on the bar wall beside bottles of whisky and gin.

She turned back to the bar, opened a bottle of diet tonic, and confided, "I'm staying in a room upstairs at the moment. It's like old times. Boyfriend trouble. You know the sort of thing."

"I'm sorry about that," said Keya, using her fork to delve into the macaroni cheese.

"I'm used to it. I've always had turbulent relationships with men. A shrink would say it stems from my childhood, but they blame everything on that. I just go for the wrong type, that's all."

Keya sipped her tea before asking, "What will you do when Coll gets back?"

"I'm looking for somewhere to lodge, but it's really pricey in this area. I think I'll need to find another job to cover the cost, or perhaps I'll move on."

"That's a shame. You seem happy here."

Kate sipped her drink and appeared to be considering Keya's comment. Finally, she muttered, "I am. I'm home. But what will be the cost of my return?"

CHAPTER TEN

On Thursday morning, Keya started her police duties by visiting old Mr Finch whose quad bike had been stolen. He must be in his eighties, but he still ran a small rundown farm with sheep and a herd of beef cattle.

Keya drove into the farmyard, unable to navigate round all the potholes which had filled up with rain the previous evening.

As she climbed out of her car, she noticed the streak of mud running across the back door and rear of the vehicle. She ought to open an account with the Polish guys who'd set up a hand car wash in a disused petrol station on the Burford Road, leading into Cirencester, but at least visiting them saved her the time of washing it herself.

"Hello, Sergeant, did I call you?" Mr Finch stopped whatever he was doing to the hinges of a metal five bar gate which he'd leaned against the breeze block wall of his barn.

"No, Mr Finch, but I heard your quad bike has been stolen, so I thought I'd follow it up."

"You won't find it, you know. It'll be packed anyway in a container ready to be shipped to who knows where."

"I'm sure you're right, but you'll still need a case number for your insurers."

"I'm not sure what they'll do. They muttered after the last one was stolen that they wouldn't insure another unless I upgraded the shed where I kept it. So I parked my car in the shed and kept the new quad bike in my garage and installed new locks. I even added an intruder alarm, which was making a right racket when I get home from my dominoes match at the King's Head."

"Do you think the thieves knew you were out?"

Mr Finch shrugged. "I usually play dominoes on a Wednesday, so it's possible."

She knew most thefts of agricultural equipment, quad bikes and 4x4 vehicles were carried out by gangs who, as Mr Finch had pointed out, exported the stolen items in shipping containers to India and the Middle East. Members of the gangs had started visiting country pubs and listening to local gossip, picking up patterns of behaviour which they could exploit.

Keya had tried to explain to farmers like Mr Finch that they should vary the times they left the farm, but many of them organised shopping, or trips to their accountants or solicitors, around market days, and these were set by the auctioneers and were usually the same day and time each week or month.

Mr Finch picked up a screwdriver. "You'll have the bike's details on file. I filled in one of your forms when I bought it."

Keya encouraged farmers to register their vehicles and larger pieces of equipment with her, so she could set up a database, which would help her when pieces were stolen. In truth, she couldn't keep up with the information she was sent, and if thefts weren't reported, it had little use anyway.

"Email the case number and I'll pass it to the insurers. And see what they say this time," suggested Mr Finch as he returned to his gate.

Keya's phone buzzed.

She turned away from Mr Finch and answered it. "Hiya, Ryan."

"The Inspector wonders if you can help with interviews today. Sergeant Unwin has got himself invited to what he calls a management seminar, although I'm sure I heard him mutter something about golf clubs."

"Sure. Where do you want to start?"

"With Rachael's brother, Nathan Fawcett. He recently bought a car showroom on the Burford Road."

"OK. It'll take me about twenty-five minutes to get there."

She finished the call as there was a metal thump and then another as Mr Finch whacked the hinge of the gate with a hammer.

"Are you off now?" he asked.

"Yes, I'm helping on another case and need to interview someone."

"Can you help me with this before you go?" He indicated towards the gate.

"Sure. What do you want me to do?"

"We need to carry it back to that pen and lift it onto the pins."

"No problem," replied Keya, picking up the latch end of the gate. It wasn't too heavy at first, but it was cumbersome to carry and several times she caught her lightweight police jacket on the triangular-shaped latch, which stuck out at the end.

"Nearly there," wheezed Mr Finch. "OK, lower it to the floor."

Gratefully, Keya did as requested.

"Now, follow my instructions to lift it back onto the pins."

Once again Keya lifted the gate and found herself moving it backwards and then forwards, and this way and that, until finally the metal hoops slipped onto the pins of the hinges.

"Thank you," said a relieved Mr Finch. "Not sure I could have done that on my own."

As they walked towards her car, Mr Finch said, "I saw you yesterday, on the telly. That was a nasty tumble you took, and even worse is that business about the skeleton. Is it the lass that went missing from The Axeman all those years ago?"

Keya stopped and asked, "How do you know about that?"

"My cousin, Rick Simmonds and his lad, Tim, they worked at Akemans. Porters, they called themselves, but they did some maintenance work and they drove an old van collecting and delivering furniture for the auctions. They were even interviewed at the time, but I don't think they knew much. Rick hadn't seen the lass since she'd been playing with Mr Carey's youngest daughter."

"Where can I find your cousin now? In case we need to question him."

"He's long gone. It was the cancer. But his boy is still around. Tim runs his own fleet of vans and trucks now, from a base just off the Burford Road, on the edge of Cirencester."

The Burford Road was a popular place today, thought Keya.

"Thanks, I might go and speak to him."

"If you do, can you ask him to look out for a second-hand quad bike?"

Keya nodded her head and climbed into her car.

Ryan was waiting for her at the hand car wash on the Burford Road.

She drew in beside him and wound down her window.

"It looks as if you need to leave your car here. Where have you been?" asked Ryan.

"A muddy farmyard and, you're right, I might as well get it cleaned. Give me a minute."

After she'd parked in a spare space and handed her car keys to one of the workers, being careful not to get sprayed by the hose he held, she climbed into Ryan's car and said, "Sorry I'm late by the way. I had to help a farmer with a gate."

Ryan raised his eyebrows at her as he drove away. Then he said, "I found out when Rachael was last seen."

"Oh, yes."

"It was in the files. Several people, including the lady who ran the post office, saw Rachael cycle through the village wearing shorts, T-shirt and a baseball cap."

"Did they say where she was heading?"

"South, towards the main Cirencester Road."

"Which would have taken her past Akemans."

"Except her bicycle was found in a ditch near an entrance to a field two hundred metres out of the village."

"Which suggests she never reached Akemans. But we know she did because her body was found there."

"Yes, so someone dumped her bike."

Ryan indicated and crossed the oncoming traffic, pulling into a smart car showroom with Range Rovers, Volvo SUVs, and other expensive cars.

"Isn't this Steve the Carman's place?" asked Keya as they climbed out.

"Who?" responded Ryan as he donned his flat black police hat with a band of black and white dicing.

A middle-aged man with a middle-aged paunch and a shiny grey suit met them. "I bought the premises from Steve. He left his partner and moved to Nottingham with a younger model."

"Typical," muttered Keya.

"I doubt you're here on personal business," the man said with a sneer.

Keya pinned her shoulders back and stepped towards him. "No, this is strictly official, Mr ?"

Nearby, a couple stopped examining the interior of a large BMW SUV and walked away.

The man with the shiny grey suit narrowed his eyes at Keya. "Nathan Fawcett. What do you want? You're scaring my customers."

Keya ignored Nathan's abrupt manner, taking a deep breath before she said in a conciliatory tone, "It's about Rachael."

"What about her?" replied Nathan, sounding perplexed.

Keya was surprised by his baffled tone. Everyone seemed to know about the discovery of the skeleton, since it had been all over the local news, and those who remembered the case had linked it to Rachael Fawcett's disappearance.

"Have you watched or listened to the local news?" asked Keya.

"No. I listen to Radio 1 in the morning. I need to keep with it and …" but his voice trailed off. "Why are you asking about her?"

"We found the body of a girl at Akemans yesterday. We won't know it's definitely Rachael until the forensic team confirms her identity."

Nathan leaned against a gold-coloured Range Rover and the colour drained from his face. He whispered, "A body. But Rachael disappeared over 30 years ago."

"It was a skeleton, actually, which is why there'll be a delay confirming it is her."

"Come to my office. I need a drink." Nathan pushed himself upright and turned towards a single-storey, glass fronted building.

Ryan raised his eyebrows at Keya as they followed Nathan back to his office, weaving between more cars. "The cheapest car I've seen is £15,000," whispered Ryan, which Keya knew was far more than either of them could afford.

She thought of her personal car, a second-hand, metallic reef-blue VW Polo which she'd given to herself as a Christmas present last year, and which she was immensely proud of.

Nathan sat down behind a large glass-topped desk with a wide white computer monitor to one side.

Stereotypically, a thin young woman, wearing a very short skirt, followed them into Nathan's office and asked, "Do you need anything?"

"A strong black coffee for me." Nathan looked at Ryan and Keya, who both shook their heads. "And I'm not to be disturbed while these officers are here."

The young woman looked worried as she left the office.

Nathan appeared to have pulled himself together as he said, "The body, or at least a skeleton, of a girl has been discovered at Akemans and you think it's Rachael?"

"We'll be looking at all missing person cases for girls and young women until the body is formally identified. But at the moment we're concentrating on Rachael," Keya said, hoping that a search through all the other cases wouldn't be necessary. "What can you tell us about her disappearance?"

Nathan leaned back in his chair and stared at the ceiling. "She was a precocious little brat, but that only encouraged my mates, who dared her to do all sorts of things, like dive off the wall at Akemans into the main river. It was a hot summer and she and her friends spent most of their time at Akemans, swimming or being spoilt by Mrs Devereux. We sometimes joined them for ice creams or a picnic. We might have been older, but why give up free food, and I remember a party where someone brought cheap two litre plastic bottles of beer and cider. We thought we were so cool."

Nathan laughed and sat up. "But Mr Dewsbury didn't, the miserable …"

Ryan coughed.

"Did he have a fight with Rachael?" asked Keya.

"Rachael, no, but he did punch Matt in the face. Broke his noise, the b …"

Ryan coughed again.

"So was that party the last time you saw your sister?"

"Oh no. She was in and out of the pub all weekend. I was working shifts, helping out my dad, and Rachael, well, she did her own thing. But Matt and I did drop her off at Akemans on the Tuesday, and we even had a swim ourselves. Mrs Devereux didn't seem to mind, even though Gilly wasn't there. Mousey Katherine was, of course, which meant Mr Dewsbury got annoyed and started shouting at us, so Matt and I left."

Nathan placed his hands on his desk. "That was the last time I saw her. Matt, Sam, and I drove to Devon for a party, and we weren't back until Thursday evening. I went to find Rachael, to tell her all about it, but she wasn't around. Mum and Dad were both busy, and neither of them knew when they'd last seen her. She'd just disappeared."

Nathan tapped his fingers on the glass desk. "I wondered if it was my fault, if Rachael had tried to follow me. She begged me to take her to the party, but I couldn't, she was only twelve. But if she'd decided to make her own way to us, where would she have got money for the bus and train?"

CHAPTER ELEVEN

Keya and Ryan left Nathan Fawcett to be comforted by his strong black coffee, which they suspected he might flavour with something alcoholic, and his slim, long-legged assistant.

"Did we learn much, do you think?" asked Ryan.

"I'm not sure he told us anything we won't find in the files, but it's always useful to hear what a witness has to say. And that's why I thought we might make one more visit while we're here."

"Where to?" asked Ryan.

"A transport company run by a man called Tim Simmons. My farmer this morning told me Tim and his father were porters at Akemans at the time Rachael disappeared. The company is supposed to be located somewhere around here."

Ryan removed his phone from his pocket and tapped and swiped until he said, "A quarter of a mile further out of town. On a small industrial estate."

They found TS Transport at the end of a row of corrugated metal buildings. It had a large concrete parking area surrounded by a robust-looking metal fence, with signs attached telling them to beware of the dogs. Keya thought Mr Finch's insurers would approve.

They walked towards the building, which had a large green sign attached to it with TS Transport printed in white letters. Before they reached the entrance, a trolley propelled itself out from underneath a green van and a man wearing overalls with streaks of oil across his face stared up at them.

"What do you want?" he asked gruffly.

"We're here to see Mr Simmons?" replied Keya.

"Junior or Senior?"

"Mr Tim Simmons," Keya clarified.

"That's me. So what do you want?"

"It's about a girl who went missing when you were working at Akemans."

"Is this about the skeleton they found?" The man's voice had softened.

"It is," Keya confirmed.

Tim Simmons stood up and thought about offering them his hand but instead he wiped it on a rag, that looked like an old tea towel, hanging out of his pocket.

"Crying shame when she disappeared. I know she could be a little minx, and she liked playing pranks on me. I was a nervous lad back then. But she meant no harm in it. It was hot that summer and I was so jealous of her and Gilly, and their other friend, the Dewsbury girl, larking about in the river."

"What did you think happened to her?" asked Ryan.

"I was the one who found her bike, in the ditch. I was cycling back from Akemans when I spotted it on the Thursday evening. And as I told the police back then, I swore it wasn't there in the morning."

"Did you see Rachael that Thursday?" asked Ryan.

"No, the last time I saw her was a couple of days before, when Mr Dewsbury was tearing strips off that timid daughter of his for hanging out with Rachael's brother and his friends. I felt sorry for her. It was no wonder her mother ran off with a soldier."

"And you didn't see Rachael again?" Keya pressed.

"I didn't see any of them again. Rachael disappeared and Mr Dewsbury and his daughter left."

"Was that a surprise to you, the Dewsburys leaving?" queried Keya.

"Nah. He was fed up doing other people's bidding, and Mr Carey had had enough and given him notice. He was unreliable, and I'd been doing some maintenance work with him, so I took it over. I think he'd found himself a job managing a mill in the north of Scotland."

Keya was considering if there was anything else she should ask when Ryan said, "So you took over the maintenance of the grounds at Akemans?"

"I did."

"When you were working around the back of the mill and beside the river, did you ever see any sign of Rachael, dead or alive, or anything which might have belonged to her?"

Tim Simmons dropped his eyes and kicked at a rogue stone with his boot. "I had no idea she was down there. In the old water channel. And I don't think anyone climbed onto the stone bridge or wall again that summer. The weather turned wetter and colder in August."

"Thank you for your help," said Keya. "And one more thing. Your uncle, if that's what you call Mr Finch, has had another quad bike stolen. He asked if you could look out for another second-hand one for him."

Tim groaned. "I told him to park it in the garage. We upgraded the security on it especially."

"He did," Keya confirmed. "But the thieves are getting bolder."

Ryan handed Tim Simmons one of his cards and said, "In case you remember anything else."

As they wandered back to Ryan's squad car, Keya said, "You know who we should speak to next?"

Ryan's stomach grumbled. "I was rather hoping for lunch."

"Well, if she's at home, we might be able to have that too."

"If who's at home?"

"Aunt Beanie. She must have been working at Akemans that summer, as both Gilly and Nathan Fawcett told us she provided treats for the girls. That means she knew Rachael. I'll give her a call."

Aunt Beanie answered, "Keya, how lovely to hear from you. It's very naughty of you not to visit Norman and me just because Dotty's not around."

"I'm sorry. I've been busy sorting out the cafe with Gilly, and her architect and builders," Keya replied.

"Oh, I know it's very exciting, although finding poor Rachael's body is very upsetting."

"You've heard?"

"Of course I have! And Ozzie popped round for coffee this morning to talk to me about it."

Keya moved the phone away from her face and muttered to Ryan, "Ozzie beat us to it to interview Aunt Beanie."

Ryan smiled ruefully as Keya heard Aunt Beanie ask, "So when are you coming to see us?"

"Actually," Keya began, "how about right now? And Ryan is with me."

There was a slight pause. Then Aunt Beanie enquired in a serious tone, "So that'll be in an official capacity."

Keya glanced at Ryan again before responding, "Let's just say it's an excuse to drop in, and as it's lunchtime, we can make it a more social visit."

Aunt Beanie laughed. "Especially if we're sitting at the kitchen table with something to eat. I know, I'll warm the quiches I bought at a local fundraiser yesterday, and I'll let Norman know you're coming. He's working at the moment."

Keya finished the call and turned to Ryan. "That's sorted. I better fetch my car and we'll go separately, just in case I'm called away to search for some missing sheep or something."

CHAPTER TWELVE

Keya arrived before Ryan at Meadowbank Farm on the outskirts of Fairford, a small Cotswold town. Aunt Beanie's husband, known to Keya as Uncle Cliff, had farmed at Meadowbank all his life, as had generations of the Devereux family before him.

But he and Aunt Beanie didn't have children and, when he developed dementia and was unable to continue farming, a contractor was brought in to work the farm.

Aunt Beanie still retained some of the farm buildings and a small paddock in front of the house where Norman Climpson kept his cow, Buttercup. Norman had moved into the large three-storey Cotswold stone farmhouse at the same time as Dotty had taken over the adjoining farm cottage.

He'd helped Aunt Beanie care for Uncle Cliff until Uncle Cliff had a fall and it became clear it wasn't safe for him to remain at home. After a short period recovering in the local community hospital, he'd moved to a residential home on the edge of Burford, a nearby Cotswold town.

Norman remained at Meadowbank Farm, providing company for Aunt Beanie, and undertaking maintenance and other jobs around the house and the part of the farm she'd retained. He also worked as the porter at Akemans.

As Keya climbed out of her car, Ryan drove into the broken

concrete yard and parked between her car and an old boxy-style green Range Rover.

"We're not the only visitors," said Keya as Ryan climbed out of the squad car clutching a bunch of red and yellow tulips.

"That's a good idea," remarked Keya. Why did she never remember those little touches?

She pushed opened a narrow metal gate and walked along an uneven flagstone path between single-storey outbuildings. Without knocking, as nobody ever did, she entered the house and halted in surprise.

Ryan side-stepped around her and also stopped, staring around. "Wow, who's cleaned up in here?" he asked.

They were used to clutter in the entrance area with an uneven row of boots and wellies and piles of coats hanging from each hook on the wall. But a wooden shoe rack now held a collection of outdoor shoes and ankle boots, with longer boots and rubber wellies upturned on the wooden rods of a boot stand.

There were far fewer coats on the wall hooks, although Keya smiled when she spotted Aunt Beanie's faded but colourful patchwork wool coat. An old, frayed armchair, which had occupied a corner position, had been removed, as had an abandoned gardening project. In their place there was a small wooden table holding a pot of hyacinths and a photograph frame of a smiling couple.

Keya moved closer and, leaning down, saw that it was a younger version of Aunt Beanie with Uncle Cliff. It was easy to spot Aunt Beanie, even though her light brown hair had now turned white, as her trademark was a colourful headscarf tied at a jaunty angle on top of her head.

"I prefer Aunt Beanie with her headscarf than the 80s style in that photo of Gilly's," remarked Ryan as Keya heard a door open.

"Oh, I agree. That perm was ghastly. I've no idea what possessed me, but they were all the rage." Today Aunt Beanie was wearing a brown scarf with images of birds on it. "I thought I heard a car, so what are you two doing loitering about in here?"

Ryan stepped forward and handed Aunt Beanie the tulips. "We were admiring the work you've done. It's very neat and tidy."

"That's Norman, not me," dismissed Aunt Beanie as she turned and walked back into the main house. "Now he's talking about painting it." She stopped and turned back. "Thank you for the flowers. They're lovely."

Ryan blushed as they entered the large, bright kitchen. The business end was near the door with a racing green Aga range cooker, a wooden shaker style kitchen, and a stainless steel sink and drainer beneath a small side window. But most of the light came from a conservatory style extension with roof lights and floor to ceiling windows.

An elderly gentleman Keya had seen at Akemans, but never been formally introduced to, was sitting at the large, rectangular pine table which was in the centre of the kitchen.

He had a round, ruddy face, either from time spent outdoors or from alcohol, or perhaps both thought Keya, noting the cut-glass tumbler in front of him, and the distinctive smell of whisky from its straw-coloured contents.

The man peered at her and Ryan from under large bushy eyebrows and barked, "Beanie, you didn't tell me the police were coming."

"Yes, I did," replied Aunt Beanie brightly, as she placed a small white milk jug and floral-patterned teacups on the table. "I said Keya and Ryan were coming for lunch and wanted to discuss the Fawcett girl, Gilly's young friend, who disappeared that hot summer."

The man grunted.

"Keya, Ryan, can I introduce my grizzly younger brother, Marmaduke Carey?"

Ryan, who had removed his hat when they entered the kitchen - Keya had left hers in her car - clasped it beneath his left arm and offered his right hand to Marmaduke. "Nice to meet you, sir."

Begrudgingly, Marmaduke shook it as he grunted something Keya couldn't catch.

Aunt Beanie placed a teapot with the image of a cow on it on the table and suggested, "Let's have a cup of tea, while we discuss business, and then we can relax over lunch. It's Earl Grey, I hope that's alright?"

At the mention of Earl Grey, Keya automatically glanced towards the Aga, expecting to see Dotty's large grey cat curled up beside it. But of course, he was in France with his owner.

The tea had an unmistakable floral aroma and taste, although it was pleasantly bitter rather than sweet.

Marmaduke refused a cup of tea and instead picked up his glass tumbler. He mused, "She was rather annoying, that Rachael. Forever vying for attention or playing practical jokes. I remember one hysterical customer who thought the girl had deliberately eaten a fly. It turned out she pretended to swat one and then swallowed a raisin. She thought it terribly funny, as did Gilly and their other little friend, but it took me forever to calm the woman down."

Aunt Beanie burst out laughing. "That was old Mrs Wriggly. And if you're talking about attention seeking, she was forever trying to get yours. I'm sure she fancied you."

"Don't be ridiculous," boomed Marmaduke.

Ryan glanced at Keya and raised his eyebrows.

"Anyway, I wasn't at all surprised when she vanished. Run away, I thought, lulled into thinking she could find a more glamorous life outside the village." Marmaduke sipped from his glass.

Aunt Beanie cradled her china cup, decorated with intertwining roses. She looked serious and said in an unemotional tone, "And she might have, a few years later."

Keya looked at Aunt Beanie and asked, "So what did you think had happened to her?"

The older women sighed. "I'm afraid I thought she'd got herself trapped somewhere, or fallen in a well or a hole and couldn't escape. Which I guess is true, although Ozzie thought there might be more to her death. That someone else was involved."

Ryan cleared his throat. "I'm afraid we won't know until the pathologist has completed his examination."

"But it is possible she was murdered?" Aunt Beanie pressed.

Keya bit her lip before replying hesitantly, "It is. But you knew her, and those working at Akemans back then. Do you think any of them could have harmed her?"

"It was none of our lot," barked Marmaduke.

"You can't know that," chided Aunt Beanie, "but Marmaduke is right. I can't think of any reason one of our employees would harm her. Although you could speak to Tim Simmonds. He was only a lad himself back then, and he's done well for himself and now runs a haulage business. His is one of the companies we recommend buyers use after an auction."

"Thanks, we spoke to him just before we came here. And we spoke to Rachael's brother, Nathan," explained Keya.

"Has he bought Steve the Carman's business?" asked Aunt Beanie.

Keya nodded, "And very proud of it he is too. All high-end models now. Nothing any of us could afford."

Marmaduke grunted, but Aunt Beanie ignored him.

"Surely Nathan didn't have anything to do with his sister's death. I wouldn't say he was particularly friendly towards her - there was a five-year age gap - but he and his friends tolerated her."

"We don't have any reason to suspect he did." Keya turned to Ryan. "But then we can't see why any of the potential suspects would have harmed her. Take yourselves, were you questioned?"

"We were, but we couldn't tell them much more than we're telling you now. Marmaduke was busy with the auction and renovating the main flour mill. We were going to extend the auction house into it at one time. As I've said, I thought Rachael was stuck somewhere, but we all searched the mill and couldn't find her."

"That's right," agreed Marmaduke. "And of course, Tim found her bike in a ditch and, as people in the village said they saw her riding it our way, we thought she hadn't reached us, so we stopped looking and got back to work."

Aunt Beanie turned to her brother. "But you still tried to use it as an excuse not to stay with your family at the beach that weekend."

He sneered at her. "But you wouldn't let me and made sure I went. I hated that guest house."

Keya looked from Marmaduke to Aunt Beanie. "Since we now know she was at Akemans, unless another young girl went missing and ended up buried on your property, is there anything you can think of which you didn't tell the police at the time?"

The two older people sadly shook their heads.

"If only we could," Aunt Beanie said despondently.

CHAPTER THIRTEEN

Aunt Beanie stood up and carried the teapot from the pine kitchen table to the worktop beside the sink in Meadowbank Farmhouse.

Keya followed with the china teacups and as she placed them next to the teapot, she admired a jam jar of wildflowers on the windowsill above the sink.

Aunt Beanie whispered to her, "Have you heard from Dotty?"

"Yes, she sent me a postcard from a place called Aix-en-Provence, which was home to a famous French painter."

"Cezanne," confirmed Aunt Beanie.

"That's the one. She's been visiting his studio and exhibitions of his paintings. And she said both she and Earl Grey are enjoying the French food."

"I'll bet Earl Grey is. Just as long as he doesn't get any fatter. Did she say anything about coming home?"

Keya shook her head.

"Well if she's happy, that's the main thing. She'll come back when she's ready."

Keya wasn't fooled by Aunt Beanie's brave smile. She clearly missed Dotty as much as Keya did.

"Let's get lunch, and then I want to hear all about the cafe. I hope this current matter doesn't delay your opening."

Keya carried plates to the table and then two bowls of salad. One with lettuce leaves, slices of cucumber and halved green grapes, and the other with grated carrots and chopped onions, tomatoes and olives.

As she placed the salads on the table, she heard Marmaduke tell Ryan, "I bought the mill in 1975. They stopped using it in the sixties and it had fallen into disrepair with trees growing into the part that's now the auction house. It had had various functions over the years ..."

Keya left the table and returned to Aunt Beanie, who was removing a baking tray and quiche from the oven.

"This is the meat one," explained Aunt Beanie, placing the metal tray on a glass, heatproof mat. "The roasted vegetable one is on a plate over there. And can you take cutlery and knives to cut them both?"

Keya returned to the pine table as Marmaduke said, "I finally persuaded the council to repair the bridge over the River Coln so that the village and, more importantly for me, the mill, were easily accessible to Cirencester and the upgraded A417."

"Here we are," Aunt Beanie announced as she placed the second quiche on its brightly coloured plate on the table. "And you're not boring Ryan, are you Marmaduke?"

"No, he's not," enthused Ryan. "It's fascinating to hear about the history of Akemans and the old mill."

Keya glanced at Ryan, but his round boyish face was sincere.

"Meat or vegetable quiche, Ryan?" asked Aunt Beanie.

"Oh, meat please."

Aunt Beanie cut him and Marmaduke generous slices of quiche as Marmaduke continued his history lesson of Akemans.

"I removed the tree and knocked out all the partitions in what is now the main auction room. Apart from the one that separates the smaller room where we can display valuable items like silver and jewellery. And I built a wall to create an office and reception area at the front. And that's where I started Akemans from."

"We started," corrected Aunt Beanie as she passed Marmaduke his plate of quiche. "You might have sorted out the building, and you definitely have business acumen, but you knew nothing about antiques back then. Sometimes I wished I'd stayed in London. It was such a glamorous lifestyle."

"In the 60s no doubt, but surely the 70s were rather grim?" countered Marmaduke.

Aunt Beanie wrinkled her nose.

"And if you hadn't come back to help me, you and Cliff wouldn't have married."

"That's very true," agreed Aunt Beanie, brightening. "And I did enjoy playing aunt to Gilly and George."

Ryan opened his mouth, but Keya stared at him and shook her head. She didn't think today was the time to ask about Aunt Beanie not having children.

"So WE started a small auction house. Our parents knew plenty of well-to-do people in the area and some of them were starting to pass away, so we persuaded their families to sell unwanted items through us. At first, anything valuable was sent to the major auction houses in London, but steadily our reputation grew, and some people only wanted to deal with one company, so the quality of sale items improved."

Marmaduke stopped speaking and spooned chopped salad onto his plate.

Keya cut a slice of the vegetarian quiche and smelt the slightly charred aroma of roasted vegetables.

"But gradually the storerooms filled up with items we hadn't sold, and which people didn't want back." Marmaduke picked up his knife and fork.

"And I couldn't bear to throw anything away," cut in Aunt Beanie. "So I persuaded Marmaduke to tackle the flour mill." She also cut a slice of the roasted vegetable quiche.

Marmaduke finished chewing and added, "It needed sorting. Vegetation was growing up the walls and damaging the stonework, but it was amazing inside. Old mill equipment had been left, and we gave most of it away to a heritage museum which was opening nearby. I cleared an area on the ground floor and built some toilets and storerooms, and Beanie created attractive displays of the items which hadn't sold. And then a local man who collected Victoriana pieces said his wife wanted to move to a bungalow and was insisting he sell most of his collection. He asked if he could have a stall in the mill and sell his pieces."

"And that was the start of what is now the antiques centre," finished Aunt Beanie.

There was silence while they all ate and then Aunt Beanie continued, "I was delighted the girls wanted to be part of the business. I worked with Gilly and handed her the reins of the antique centre, oh I think it was twelve years ago, which is when I joined the police and started working on antique-related crimes. But it took longer to pry my brother away from the auction house."

Aunt Beanie stared down the table at Marmaduke.

"And now I'm back," he replied.

"You are?" queried Keya.

"George can't run things on her own and she needs an expert around the place." Marmaduke squared his shoulders.

Aunt Beanie raised her eyebrows and said in a flat voice, "Which is why I agreed to help out."

Keya glanced from one sibling to the other, and felt the tension rise between them. "So you're both helping George. I think that's great."

Aunt Beanie turned to her and smiled. "And we might need your assistance again at the next auction."

Keya had agreed to help out at March's busy auction, as Akemans had been short staffed. And Gilly had asked her again in April as Dotty was away, but she wasn't sure she wanted to make it a regular commitment.

"George thinks we should find a new receptionist, but Gilly's arguing that we should wait to see what Dotty wants to do," explained Aunt Beanie. "Personally, I think we should find someone because, even when Dotty does return, she'll be able to do more of the valuation work. But you'll have time to help this month, Keya? The cafe won't be ready."

"No, the building work isn't due to finish until the 10th of June but it's likely to be delayed now," Keya replied.

"Why?" Ryan asked. "Is the cafe opening dependent on refurbishing the waterwheel?"

"I'm not sure." Keya looked across the table at him, "But I bet the builders use the police presence as an excuse. I'm sure they're already behind their projected schedule."

"Why do you think that?" asked Aunt Beanie.

"They haven't started plasterboarding the internal walls. It's still what they call a 'shell', and I don't think we can knock out the hole for the windows overlooking the waterwheel while the channel is still a crime scene."

"I can see that," agreed Aunt Beanie.

"What's that about holes in walls?" asked Marmaduke.

"We want to create a feature of the waterwheel as I found a grant to fund its renovation. So we're creating a large window, so cafe customers can view it. But it means knocking out a section of the external wall."

"Just you be careful," warned Marmaduke. "You never know what you might uncover when you start messing about with old buildings."

CHAPTER FOURTEEN

Keya didn't return to Cirencester police station after lunch at Meadowbank Farm. An alarm on her phone reminded her she had a meeting with the Lechlade Music Festival committee.

The popular music festival was taking place later in the month and they wanted her advice on crowd control and preventing drug-related deaths, which had occurred at other music festivals the previous year. But Keya knew it was almost impossible to prevent such tragic cases.

Driving back home after the meeting, she realised she hadn't been to the supermarket and the contents of her fridge were woefully low.

Her phone buzzed in its holder attached to the windscreen and she saw the caller was Ryan.

Answering it, she said, "Have you made much headway with the case?"

"Some, and I know you're off tomorrow, so can I come round this evening and discuss it?"

Keya thought of her fridge. She'd restock it tomorrow.

"It'll have to be the pub again. I've no food in the house, but we better make it early, or the cook will have left."

After showering and changing into jeans, T-shirt and the sweatshirt she'd been given by the Lechlade Music committee that afternoon, Keya wandered into the village and entered the Dog and Duck.

"Hiya," she called across to Kate, who was standing behind the bar, reading a newspaper.

Several tables were full, mostly with couples but in the corner, by the fireplace, a family with three young children were enjoying a meal.

Ryan was sitting opposite Derek and Bernard and as he turned to see Keya, his gaze rose to the ceiling.

Keya narrowed her eyes as she approached their table and demanded, "Have you been harassing my friend?"

"Not us," replied Derek, shaking his head with feigned innocence.

"But it's his round," announced toothless Bernard, raising his glass.

"No, it isn't," called Kate without lifting her eyes from the newspaper. "He bought the last one."

"Worth a try," cackled Bernard, nudging Derek.

"Nice talking to you," said Ryan politely, as he stood up and joined Keya. Together, they approached the bar.

In the paper Kate was reading, Keya saw a large picture of Nathan Fawcett, standing in front of his car showroom. "Good advertising," she observed.

"He seems genuinely upset about his missing sister," muttered Kate. "And it's been so long." She looked up at them and asked, "Are you the police officers it says interviewed him this morning?"

Ryan nodded.

"Who wrote the article?" asked Keya, but she thought she knew.

Kate checked the name under the headline. "Ozzie Winters."

"Now how did she know about our interview?" Keya looked at Ryan.

His eyes widened. "I didn't say anything. Besides, interviewing the victim's brother is the most logical first step."

Keya wasn't convinced, but there was nothing she could do at the moment.

"How was he, Nathan?" asked Kate.

"Do you know him?" asked Keya in surprise.

"I did, but that was another life."

"He's done well for himself," said Ryan. "He has a large house in an exclusive residential estate on the outskirts of Cirencester and two showrooms selling luxury used cars."

"Can we have the dominoes, pet?" asked a stooped man, leaning on a wooden walking stick. He had wispy grey hair and looked every one of his advanced years.

"Of course, Arthur." Kate reached under the bar counter. "And your usual?"

"Yes, please," replied the elderly man.

"I'll bring it over."

"What about us?" shouted Bernard.

"You two need to pay for your drinks first," Kate called back. She turned to Keya and Ryan and asked, "Are you eating?"

"Yes, please," replied Keya as she took the two menus Kate handed her.

"The special is steak and chips," Kate told them. "The butcher delivered some lovely pieces of sirloin this afternoon."

"I'll have that," replied Ryan. "Medium rare."

"Excellent, and I know Coll's sister was talking about sweetcorn fritters. I'll see if she's made the batter. But first, what would you like to drink?" asked Kate.

Keya and Ryan carried their drinks across to a free table between the family who were finishing their meal and the three old friends who'd tipped the box of black and white dominoes onto the table between them.

When they were seated, Keya asked, "Do you really think it's pure coincidence that Ozzie interviewed Nathan Fawcett so soon after us?"

"At least it was after us and not before," responded Ryan, before supping his pint of zero alcohol beer. He placed his glass back on the table, on a rectangular beer mat advertising a brand of lager, and added, "But no, I don't think it's a coincidence. But short of checking my car for a bug or tracking device, I'm not sure what to do."

Keya scowled. "Maybe she does have a way of tracking us. Let's see if it happens again. So what did you discover this afternoon?'

"I've been working through the file and making phone calls. One of the lodgers from the pub is dead and another, a regular who'd stayed there two nights a week for the whole of the year prior to Rachael's disappearance, is in a nursing home with Alzheimer's. Although he may remember more about what happened thirty years ago than the last three days, the staff weren't optimistic he could add any more to the statement he made at the time."

"Sounds reasonable," considered Keya.

"I spoke to the other regular, and he said he rarely saw Rachael, as he worked in his room at night and was out during the day. He couldn't remember when he'd last seen her. And I checked through the file and his movements that week were all accounted for, with witnesses."

"So that's everyone who was staying at the pub?"

"No. The man who was house hunting. Clearly someone spoke to him at the time, as they added the note about that, but I can't track him down and there is nothing on file about his movements the week Rachael disappeared. I'll see what else I can find out tomorrow. And Sergeant Unwin will be back to help."

"Has Rachael's identity been confirmed?"

"Not yet, we're still waiting." Ryan sipped his pint and then asked, "How did the dress fitting go last night?"

Keya beamed at him. "My outfit is gorgeous. I was really worried I'd have to wear a sari or something awful, but my sister, Zivah, chose a wonderful pale turquoise-blue jacket and skirt."

"I bet you'll look stunning."

Keya realised she was blushing.

"Here you are," said Kate as she placed a large oval plate of steak, thick-cut chips and peas in front of Ryan, and a stack of fritters with a creamy-looking dip on the table for Keya.

"It's my day off tomorrow and as Coll's sister is looking after the bar, we won't be serving food," Kate told them.

"It's my day off too," said Keya, picking up a warm crisp fritter. She was about the dunk it into the dip when she stopped and asked, "So why don't you come to mine for supper? That is, if you don't mind vegetarian food."

Kate smiled warmly. "I'm happy with any food if someone else is cooking. That sounds' wonderful. You're just up the street, aren't you?"

"Yes, next to Derek and Peggy. Shall we say seven?"

"I can't wait." Kate turned and left them to enjoy their meal.

CHAPTER FIFTEEN

Keya had learnt that if she had a lie-in, and a late start to her day off, she accomplished little so she was up and about by eight o'clock on Friday morning.

Whilst munching a piece of toast, having cut the mouldy edge off the bread, she wrote a shopping list on the back of an old envelope.

What to cook for Kate that evening? Something which represented the food she wanted to serve in her cafe. But it had to be more than vegetarian sausage rolls and cakes.

She stood up and walked across to an upright shelving unit where she kept her cookery books and removed a pink file with pictures of cupcakes on it. It contained recipes she'd printed out or cut from magazines and filed away, and several plastic wallets held smaller cuttings.

At the front, several sheets of lined paper held notes she'd made about her menu. She wanted to avoid fast food items like burgers and hot dogs. Other cafes she'd visited served crisps, coleslaw, and a small salad instead of fries, and this was her preferred route.

Sandwiches would be one section of her menu with some standard ones like ham, egg mayonnaise, and a local cheese with chutney or mustard. But she also wanted to rotate through some special fillings to keep the menu fresh.

Maybe this week she should prepare variations on a chicken sandwich. She sipped her tea as she emptied one of the plastic wallets onto her small drop-leaf oak kitchen table.

Sifting through the notes and clippings she found recipes for coronation chicken, which had a mild curry and apricot or mango flavouring; chicken tikka, which was spicier with turmeric, cayenne and coriander; and chicken Caesar, which was a variation on the salad with grilled chicken, crispy lettuce, shavings of parmesan cheese, and capers or anchovies.

She wrote down ingredients for the various sandwiches on her shopping list.

But she still hadn't decided what to cook this evening. Keep it simple. Soup? No. Grilled halloumi? Possibly, with a salad or couscous. Or a quiche or tart?

How about trying the recipe from the *Artichoke* food magazine for a cherry tomato tart tatin using shortcrust pastry rather than puff, because it said it soaked up the juices better? She could make her own shortcrust pastry, and the tomatoes would work well with halloumi. A fresh tart tatin on a hot summer day might sell well.

She finished her list, washed up her breakfast things and, grabbing her bags, climbed into her VW Polo. She drove steadily to Cirencester, singing away to music from the 1990s and 2000s on the local radio station.

After completing her shopping at a supermarket on the edge of town, she drove into Cirencester and parked at the Forum car park, close to the police station. She hoped she wouldn't bump into any of her colleagues, but just in case, she stuffed her two steamy romance books into her bright patchwork sling bag and walked to the library.

The library wasn't busy but two other women, one of them a mum with a toddler sitting in a pushchair reading a picture book, were examining the spicier end of the romance books. She smiled self-consciously as she also looked through the selection. She'd already read many of the books, and she felt like a change.

Moving around the end of the aisle, she found a small section dedicated to paranormal romance books. That was something she hadn't tried before, and she was surprised to find it in Cirencester library as she thought the town's inhabitants were too conservative to read such books.

Another woman joined her and pulled out two books on the second shelf down.

"Shifter romance," she explained. "I enjoyed the first one, so I thought I'd try the rest of the series."

"Shifter romance?" queried Keya.

"Oh, you must try it. It's such fun. Here, start with this one." The lady removed a book with a black and purple cover and the image of a young woman, wearing what looked like leather or latex, a howling wolf, and the full moon.

Hesitantly, Keya took the book from the smiling woman, who said, "I must go. I'm teaching in ten minutes."

Keya shook her head and smiled. If a teacher had suggested the book, how could she refuse? But she also took two more books from the main romance section. One was a mafia romance and the other a lighter-hearted romantic comedy.

After checking the books out, she glanced at her watch. She still had an hour until her meeting at Akemans with Gilly, Gilly's architect, and Vic Peters. Just the excuse she needed to have a cup of tea.

She tried to find different cafes and had recently expanded her search away from central Cirencester to other locations. This morning the church in Kemble was holding a fundraiser in its church hall with a few stalls, and the local ladies serving teas and coffees to visitors.

Even though she was off duty, she knew attending such events was appreciated by the local community, so she decided to go.

Just over an hour later, Keya parked at Akemans. Beside her on the passenger seat was a paper plate, carefully wrapped in a plastic bag, holding a selection of cakes, bakes and scones the women at the church had insisted she take. She'd enjoyed her cheese scone at the church, although she wasn't sure it had complemented her cup of Earl Grey tea.

Feeling guilty about being given so many cakes, she'd bought four books for £1 at the bookstall. She'd been surprised to find a steamy-looking historical romance and when she picked it up, the lady running the stall, who was in her fifties, cried with delight and found her all four books in the series. Keya wondered if the lady was the one who'd donated them.

"Sorry I'm late," she said as she joined Gilly, Fergal, the architect, and Vic Peters in the builders' breakout area at the back of the old flour mill.

"Tea or coffee?" asked Vic.

"No thanks, I've just had one at Kemble church hall."

"Supporting the local community," noted Gilly. "Well done, people appreciate it and are more likely to help you out. The cafe will need regular local customers to keep it going during the winter months."

"So where are you with your schedule?" asked Fergal, an Irish twang to his voice.

"The ground works have been done outside, and the foundations started on the extension," Vic replied. "We've been delayed inside as we found some old wiring which wasn't safe so we're having to install a completely new ring main for the cafe. I spoke to Gilly about it," said Vic.

Gilly nodded. "I've no idea who my father got in to do the original work, but it looks as if we'll have to sort out the rest of the wiring in the antiques centre after we've finished with the cafe."

"And we can't knock out the external wall until the police give us the go ahead," said Vic. "It's likely to delay completion of the project."

Keya had expected him to say that.

"Not necessarily," countered Fergal. "There will be no plasterboard on the external wall, as we're leaving the stonework exposed. Finish tidying it up and repoint it as per the schedule and then we'll see where we are with the windows."

They discussed other aspects of the building work until Fergal suggested, "Shall we look outside at the extension?"

Keya viewed the trenches which had been dug into the dark soil and remarked, "It doesn't look very big."

"Don't worry, buildings always look small at this stage," reassured Fergal. "Just wait until the walls have been built, plastered, and painted. It will look much larger then. Have you thought whether you want any permanent shelves building, or are you going to have shelves you can move around?"

Keya bit her lip. The fitting out of the shop and cafe, which was the term Fergal and the builders used, was something Keya couldn't get her head around and she found it rather daunting.

"I'm not sure," she replied, knowing her answer was vague.

"If you do want Vic and his team to make some, you'll need to tell us by the end of next week. I left a gap in the schedule and some money in the budget for them if you do."

Gilly touched Keya's arm. "Come and see me at the beginning of the week and we'll go through it. I know a bit about arranging stalls and shops from working in the antiques centre."

"Thank you," replied Keya with relief.

Vic was staring over Keya's shoulder towards the riverbank. "Who's that?" he asked.

Keya turned as a figure wearing a tweed jacket pulled a matching cap low over their head and scuttled away from the stone bridge, along the riverbank.

"It doesn't look like a reporter," Fergal commented.

"It could be one of my dad's friends," considered Gilly, "but if it is, why are they acting so suspiciously?"

"Brad," called Vic.

The older man appeared wearing a high-vis jacket and his yellow hard hat.

"Go and see what that fellow wants," instructed Vic, pointing to the tweed back of the figure moving away from them.

Fergal and Vic returned to the open foundation trenches. "Any problems with the ground?" asked Fergal.

"Only the old rubbish pit we found, but we dug it out and poured concrete into the hole," Vic replied. "We've just about finished over there."

He pointed to the far trench where a brick wall was visible, level with the ground. "And the rest should be completed by Tuesday. Then we'll lay the floor and leave it to dry while we continue inside. Hopefully, the police will allow us to knock out that hole then." He looked across at Keya and raised his eyebrows.

She smiled back thinly in response.

"Now who's that?" asked Vic, in an exasperated tone.

Another figure, slim, and possibly a woman, had appeared, walking past the end of the auction house building, heading towards the river. They wore boots and jeans with a dark padded jacket and a beanie hat.

"Hey, this is a building site," shouted Vic. "There's no access to the public." The figure lifted a hand in acknowledgement but continued on their course.

Vic sighed, reached for his mobile phone and called Brad. "When you've finished with the first visitor, we've another, heading for the river. Can you escort whoever it is away from our building site?" He finished his call and said, "Shall we finish off inside?"

Fergal and Gilly followed him into the mill, but Keya hesitated, watching the second figure standing beside the river. There was something familiar about them.

Then she spotted Brad in his high-vis jacket and yellow hard hat and the figure turned towards him. They seemed to consider each other before the figure turned and dashed back the way they'd come.

Keya waited while Brad wandered back towards her. "What was that all about?"

"Young woman snooping about. Probably a reporter."

Keya thought it was just the sort of thing Ozzie Winters would do. Was she following Keya?

"And the first person?"

"I'm not sure what he wanted. He disappeared. I think I'll go and check they've both left."

Brad turned and walked away.

Keya returned home after her meeting at Akemans and after lunch, a bowl of cauliflower and kale soup she'd bought from the supermarket, she prepared to make her tomato tart tatin.

She was most concerned about the tomatoes making the pastry base soggy, so she did some research and decided to cut the cherry tomatoes in half and roast them with onions, garlic and thyme. She drizzled over some olive oil and balsamic vinegar but left out the sugar, as the small tomatoes were sweet enough.

Keya enjoyed her afternoon baking the tatin, which she'd warm up again when Kate arrived, and preparing several sandwich mixes, which she'd also ask Kate to sample.

Although today was her day off, Keya still found her thoughts drifting back to work and the current case. She hadn't heard from Ryan, which was probably good news.

At half past six, she started preparing the couscous for the salad. While she waited for the grains to plump up as they absorbed the vegetable stock she'd poured over them, she cut up a little gem lettuce and placed it in a bowl with the contents of a bag of mixed salad leaves and rocket she'd bought that day.

At seven o'clock she added pomegranate seeds, pine nuts, and mint leaves to the couscous. Next, she set the table.

At seven-fifteen she sliced the halloumi cheese and turned on the oven to warm the tatin and crisp it up.

By seven-thirty, there was nothing else she could be but wait.

At eight o'clock, she pulled on her coat and opened the front door. Perhaps Kate had been asked to work at the pub and hadn't been able to contact her.

Keya walked down the street and opened the door to the Dog and Duck. It was busier tonight, being a Friday, and several groups of people were clustered around the bar, and most of the seats around the tables were occupied too. Kate must be working.

Keya approached the bar and spotted a red-faced woman who placed a tall pint-sized glass under a brass tap, beneath a long, thin handle and a sign with Wiltshire Gold printed on it. The woman pulled the handle, and a thick dark liquid slowly filled the glass.

"Hiya, is Kate here?" Keya asked.

"I wish she was. I've left her several messages, but she hasn't called me back. I just hope she's not with that man of hers. He's a nasty piece of work."

"Oh, well. Thank you." As there was nothing else, she could do, Keya turned and left the pub. As she trudged back home, she wondered if Kate had received a better offer for this evening than having a vegetarian supper with a Hindu policewoman.

Maybe she had met up with her ex-boyfriend and they were making up for lost time.

There was one thing Keya knew. Kate wouldn't make a reliable manager for the cafe if she couldn't be relied upon to turn up.

CHAPTER SIXTEEN

What was that? Keya heard ringing. Her phone? Drowsily she reached across to her bedside table and picked it up.

"Yes," she answered groggily.

"It's Vic. You need to come to the site now."

"Which site?" she asked in bewilderment.

"The building site at Akemans. I can't say any more, but I'll meet you there. Phone this number when you arrive." Vic abruptly finished the call.

What was all that about? And what time was it?

She checked the display on her phone. 6.45 am and today was Saturday. Adrenaline kicked in. If Vic was calling this early at the weekend, when he wasn't working at the site, then something serious had happened.

Ignoring the shower, and caught up in Vic's urgency, she disregarded her jeans and civilian clothes, and instead chose her black uniform trousers and white long-sleeved shirt. She ignored her stab-proof vest but pulled on a thin black police jacket.

Grabbing her flat hat from a peg in the hall, she picked up her colourful sling bag and keys for her Ford Focus and rushed out of the door.

It was a bright but blustery day, and she wouldn't be surprised if it rained in the afternoon. She sped along the country roads, her senses heightening at every corner and twist and turn. She did meet a tractor and trailer and braked sharply, pulling onto the verge to give it room to pass.

At Akemans she parked in front of the auction house, next to a large black Toyota Hilux with S&G Builders printed on the passenger door. It reminded her to call Vic.

Before she had time to speak, Vic asked, "Are you here?"

"Yes," she replied, presuming he meant Akemans.

"Walk past the auction house to the building site and I'll meet you there."

Keya did as instructed.

As she turned the corner at the back of the auction house and looked across the building site to the old mill, she realised the site was surrounded by panels of two-metre-high metal fencing.

The panels nearest to her had always been open on her previous visits, but today Vic was lifting one of them out of its temporary concrete base. A man wearing a dark-coloured jacket and trousers, whose German Shepherd was sitting obediently beside him, seemed to be with Vic.

Keya walked towards them.

"Keya, Sergeant Varma, this is Ed Meadows, from 24Hour Security." Vic swung the metal panel open and stood back as he said, "Come through."

"What's happened?" asked Keya. "Has someone broken in and stolen your equipment, or vandalised the building?"

"I'm afraid it's worse than that," replied Vic, leading her towards the cafe extension and the trenches she'd been shown the previous day. As they approached, she saw that the foundation in the side trench had been completed and the wall was level with the ground.

"We employ 24Hour Security to check the site at night and at the weekends when we're not working. Occasionally they do find kids messing around but today his dog, Nola, found this."

Vic stepped forward and indicated for Keya to join him by the open trench of what would be the front of the cafe extension.

Keya peered in. The foundation wall was only a few courses of brickwork high. But there was a body slumped across it. A person wearing jeans, a dark blue padded blue jacket, and a beanie hat.

"Is that the same person who was on site yesterday? Who we thought was a reporter?" Keya's stomach clenched. Had someone killed Ozzie?

"It looks like it, but I haven't seen her before."

Her. Oh, no. Was it Ozzie?

"You can see her face from the other side." Vic stepped across a precarious bridge created from two planks of scaffolding.

Gingerly, Keya followed him, the planks wobbling beneath her feet as she rushed to safety and what would be her office when the extension was completed. She picked her way back along the trench until she was facing the body and then she gasped.

It wasn't Ozzie. The person lying dead in the trench, her eyes open but empty, was Kate, from the Dog and Duck.

"Do you know her?" asked Vic sharply.

"Yes," replied Keya in disbelief. "She was supposed to have supper with me last night, but she didn't show up."

"So she was a friend of yours?"

"Not exactly. She worked as a barmaid at the local pub, and I thought she might be interested in managing the cafe for me."

"Do you think she came to check it out and tripped and fell into the trench?" asked Vic, a note of relief in his voice.

"I don't see why she would. I hadn't said anything to her about the cafe, or the job. I was going to raise it last night. When she didn't arrive, and the lady helping out at the pub said she hadn't seen or spoken to her, I dismissed Kate as unreliable, and not someone I wanted to work with."

"When all along she was lying here, dying," sighed Vic.

Keya swallowed and became businesslike. "We can't make any assumptions."

"Have you finished with me?" called Ed. "It's just that Nola and I are working at the football in Cheltenham today and we both need food."

"You found the body?" Keya checked.

"Yes. I arrived at six and Nola must have sensed it straight away as she pulled me across to the trench. That's when I called Vic."

"And woke me up," confirmed the foreman.

"I'll take a formal statement from you when I've called this in."

Keya didn't have her radio with her. It was charging on its stand in the house. She would need to call someone, but who? Ryan? No, he was too junior for a suspicious death. Sergeant Unwin? She could call him, but something within her resisted. Instead, she went straight to her boss, Inspector Evans.

"Sergeant Varma," barked the inspector down the phone. At least he was awake.

"We have a situation at Akemans," Keya explained.

"Not another thirty-year-old body?" asked the inspector in a tone which almost sounded as if he was making a joke.

"No. More like a three-hour old one."

There was no mistaking the inspector's serious tone now. "You know the drill, Sergeant. Secure the scene and interview whoever found the body. I'll call SOCO and ask them to send someone straight away. It's bright now but forecast to rain later, so we need to get on with things."

He paused as if thinking before asking in a softer tone, "I don't suppose you know who the victim is? It's not anyone from Akemans is it?"

"Nobody from Akemans, sir. But I do know the victim. And she was supposed to have supper with me last night."

CHAPTER SEVENTEEN

Vic Peters left to make hot drinks as Keya started interviewing Ed Meadows, the security guard. His German Shepherd, Nola, lay on the ground at his feet, ignoring the nearby body in the trench.

"As I told you, I arrived at six o'clock for my round, as we're working at the football stadium today," repeated Ed.

"Was it obvious that someone had broken into the building site?" Keya asked.

"No, the fence was intact and the padlock still on the panel at the entrance. Nothing alerted me to intruders. Which was why I was so surprised when Nola started barking and straining at the lead. She led me straight across to the trench and stood at the top of it, continuing to bark. And that's when I looked down and saw the figure. The morning was light enough for me to see it was a slim figure, probably a woman, and that she was lying at an awkward angle." Ed paused.

"What did you do next? Did you move her?"

"No, how could I get down into the trench, or if I did, how would I get out again? I called to her and asked if she was OK and when I didn't get a response, I called Vic."

"Not the ambulance?"

Ed shook his head. "I was certain it was too late for that. The body looked … dead."

"You've seen a dead body before?"

"I was in the forces," was all he said in response.

Keya nodded in understanding.

"Can I go now?" asked Ed.

"I think so. Let me take your contact details so we can speak to you again if we need to."

Keya learned that Ed lived in Cheltenham, and he provided her with his phone number and his manager's name and contact details at 24Hour Security.

He left as Vic appeared carrying three mugs. Vic handed one to Keya and said loudly, probably so Ed could hear, "Making that extra cup of tea was a waste of effort."

"Never waste a perfectly good cup of tea," bellowed Inspector Evans, who stood on the far side of the fence, watching a young police officer Keya didn't recognise lift and open the entrance panel.

Inspector Evans nodded to Ed as he left, before striding towards Keya. Vic handed the inspector a chipped brown cup.

The inspector sipped and grimaced. "Only one sugar. Never mind, it'll have to do. Now show me this body."

The inspector, Vic, and Keya all stood on the edge of the trench, looking down.

"Won't be able to discern the victim's footprints from these others in this earth," noted the inspector. "She's definitely dead?"

"Yes, sir," confirmed Keya.

"Good, that saves the young PC who drove me climbing down into the trench to check," declared the inspector.

"I'll have nobody climbing into my crime scene," announced a white-clad figure in a challenging tone. He was carrying a pair of white boots.

"I wish I could say it's good to see you again, but I can't," Inspector Evans said flatly. "How long will you be?"

"As long as I need to be," was the curt reply as the senior SOCO also stared into the trench. "Do you need an identity?"

"I think we already know who the victim is." Inspector Evans turned to Keya and asked, "Sergeant?"

"I know her as Kate, and she worked at my local pub. But I don't know her full name," Keya replied.

The SOCO stood up and shouted across to his younger colleague, who had just entered the building site wheeling his aluminium box. "Graham, we'll need the ladder."

Graham abandoned the box, returned to a blue van and extracted an aluminium ladder. He carried it over to the group as they watched, silently, and together he and the senior SOCO extended the ladder down into the trench, placing the feet of it several metres away from the body.

The senior SOCO pulled on the boots he'd been carrying and climbed down into the trench as his younger colleague returned for the mystery aluminium box, which he struggled to pull across a patch of sticky brown earth.

Keya sipped her tea as she watched the senior SOCO working. He approached the body cautiously, searching the ground and the newly constructed foundation wall. He spotted something small and round, like a button, and stopped to pick it up, placing it in an evidence bag.

Keya had worked on many cases herself collecting evidence, and she understood his cautious approach. Eventually, he stood over the body and inserted a thermometer into its ear and then touched its hand. Keya still couldn't bring herself to identify the figure in the trench as Kate from the pub.

"Poor thing has been here all night. What time did you close the site?" asked the senior SOCO.

"I left just after four. One of my team, Brad, was tidying away, but he didn't have much left to do."

The senior SOCO removed the thermometer and, reading it, said, "Before you ask, I'd estimated she was killed between six and ten o'clock last night."

"Killed?" queried Inspector Evans.

"Yes, hit with something round. This dent in her head wasn't made when she fell into the trench."

Keya looked straight ahead, not wanting to see evidence of the blow that had killed someone she had started to think of as a friend and potential work colleague.

She continued to ignore the senior SOCO's movements in the trench below, sipping her tea as if on autopilot.

"Here's her wallet," called up the senior SOCO.

This caught Keya's attention.

"You'll have to lean down further," urged the senior SOCO to his colleague, Graham.

Graham knelt on the brown earth and reached into the trench until he grasped a spotty patterned purse. Straightening up, he handed it to the inspector, who had already pulled on a pair of blue latex gloves.

Inspector Evans opened it and from amongst several plastic cards removed a driving licence. "Our victim is Katherine Dewsbury."

Keya started, and tea from her cup sloshed into the trench.

"Oy, what are you doing?" called the senior SOCO angrily.

"Sergeant, that name mean something to you?" asked the inspector.

"Yes, it's the name of Gilly Wimsey's other childhood friend. Gilly, Katherine, and Rachael Fawcett all swam and messed around in the river here the summer Rachael disappeared."

Inspector Evans looked grim as he said, "Then this death is no coincidence."

CHAPTER EIGHTEEN

Keya didn't return home after the discovery of a second body at the cafe building site at Akemans.

Inspector Evans had instructed her to call Ryan while he contacted Sergeant Unwin to ask them both to come into the police station, despite it being Saturday morning.

Keya drove straight to Cirencester, parking in her unoccupied space outside the uninspiring rectangular police building, constructed from what she suspected was fake Cotswold stone.

Inside, the station was quiet, but she knew that would change during the day. It was liveliest on Saturday evenings, and she hoped that by then she'd be home, curled up on the sofa watching Saturday night TV.

She turned the lights on in her team's room and was just hanging her patchwork bag on the back of her chair when the tall figure of Ryan strolled in. He wore a blue top with the Cheltenham Albion football club logo.

"Do you think we're going to be here all day?" Ryan asked.

"Why?" asked Inspector Evans as he entered the room. "Do you have somewhere better to be?"

"I was going to the football match." Ryan turned to Keya, and added, "Gerald invited me to watch from his company's box."

Gerald was a friend of Ryan's and a solicitor who worked for a local firm.

Inspector Evans' face softened. "I'm sorry about that, but we're all going to be busy today. We officially have a homicide investigation, as well as a cold case, and it's critical we follow up leads before the trail grows cold."

Ryan tried to cover his disappointment, but his round, boyish face had a pained expression.

"Can you two find me two incident boards?" The inspector asked as he strode across to his office and opened the door.

Ryan and Keya found boards in a storeroom Ryan dubbed 'the room of requirements' after a similar room at Hogwarts, the fictitious magical school Harry Potter attended.

Both were filled with years of unwanted and discarded items. When they returned to their team room, each pushing a two by one and half metre grey felt-covered board, they found Sergeant Unwin at his desk.

Sergeant Unwin, known as Nick to his friends and close colleagues, and Sergeant Onion behind his back, was ruggedly handsome with thick dark hair which he'd grown longer on top and styled into a trendy quiff.

Despite his association with Chief Inspector Ringrose, who it was well known had taken early retirement in order to avoid charges of corruption and bribery, he had retained his job.

Keya and her friend, Dotty, had discussed Nick, who they thought was ambitious and naive but not dishonest. There were certainly others in the police station who didn't trust him, but Keya and Ryan had agreed that as a member of their team they had to, and they would treat him with professional courtesy.

Nick stood up as Keya and Ryan entered and Keya saw he was wearing a t-shirt and shorts with a sweatshirt thrown over his shoulders.

"Do you know what this is about?" asked Nick. "The boss called and told me to come straight here. I haven't even had time for a shower after my Parkrun at Tetbury."

"How did you get on?" asked Ryan.

"Not bad," replied Nick. "It's an interesting course but undulating and the sharp hill near the beginning of the course always gets me, particularly on the second lap. We should do one together, as a team. What do you think, Keya?"

"I'd only slow you down."

"No, you wouldn't and, anyway, that doesn't matter. The joy of parkruns is that they cater for everyone. There was a granny walking with her two grandchildren this morning."

"I'll think about it."

"When you've finished," announced Inspector Evans, "we've a murder case on our hands. Push those boards against the far wall."

Ryan and Keya did as instructed, rolling the incident boards against the partition wall which separated their office from the crime prevention team next door.

Inspector Evans approached the boards, as Keya and Ryan stood back, and pinned the name 'Rachael Fawcett' to the top of one, and Katherine Dewsbury to the top of the second. He turned to face the room.

Sergeant Unwin sat back down, while Keya pulled herself onto her desk, and Ryan leaned against his.

"What we have," began Inspector Evans, his Welsh accented voice taking on a solemn tone, "are two dead bodies at the same location, separated by a time span of thirty years."

"Thirty-one," corrected Ryan.

"Very well, thirty-one," accepted the inspector. "And my gut tells me these cases," he turned and tapped Rachael's name and then Katherine's, "are linked, and that finding Rachael's body triggered the events which led to Katherine's death. But I've no idea how or why. What do you three think connects them?"

Sergeant Unwin was first to answer. "Both bodies were found at Akemans."

"Gilly Wimsey was friends with both of them when she was a girl," suggested Ryan, hesitantly.

Keya tilted her head and said, "Which then brings in other people who knew the pair, including Aunt Beanie, Marmaduke Carey, Rachael's brother Nathan, and Tim Simmonds who was working as a porter at Akemans when Rachael disappeared. They're all people we've interviewed. Do you think our questions had anything to do with Kate's death?"

To Keya, Katherine would always be Kate, as that was the name she'd known her by. She bit her lip. What if she and Ryan had touched a nerve or reopened an old wound which had led to Kate's death?

"Something could have happened in the past, which links both deaths," Sergeant Unwin suggested, "but you didn't say much on the phone, Inspector. Can you explain exactly what you found?"

Inspector Evans looked across at Keya, raised his eyebrows, and said, "Sergeant."

Keya explained her early morning phone call from the site foreman, her visit to the site, and the discovery of Kate's body in the trench. "The senior SOCO thought she'd been killed by a blow to the head with a round object, but I think we should wait for his report to confirm that."

"But for now," clarified Inspector Evans, "we are treating her death as suspicious. Sergeant Unwin, you made a good point about past events, so I want you to see if you can find any relevant ones. PC Jenkins can bring you up to speed with the file on Rachael's disappearance since you've been," the inspector paused, Keya thought for effect, "busy for the past few days. The file is in paper format and if you need anything else, I suggest you speak to Stan Rowbottom on Monday."

"Do you really think I'll find anything?" queried Nick. "Most of the people involved are probably dead."

"It was only thirty years ago, not eighty," growled the inspector.

Ryan looked as if he was about to correct the inspector again but thought better of it and shut his mouth.

Inspector Evans stepped to one side and tapped Rachael's board. "So, Sergeant Unwin, you'll take the lead on Rachael Fawcett's death. The most pressing point is confirming her identity. Can you chase up the SOCOs on Monday for an answer?"

"Yes, sir," replied Nick flatly, and glancing at him, Keya noticed his lips pressed together and she thought he looked disappointed to be working on Rachael's case.

"Also, Sergeant," the inspector addressed Nick again, "dig around and find out more about the relationship between Rachael and

Katherine Dewsbury, and anything which happened when they were kids which might provide answers to their deaths."

Ryan asked, "Do you think we should warn Gilly Wimsey?"

Inspector Evans tilted his head back and consulted the ceiling. After a minute or so, he turned his attention to Ryan and replied, "I don't think so, but you and Keya should speak to her anyway, after we're finished here, and perhaps you should caution her to be careful."

Inspector Evans stepped in front of Rachael's board and tapped Katherine's. "Which takes us on to today's case. Sergeant Varma, as you knew the deceased, and some of her recent history, I want you to take the lead. But as you also have other engagements in your role as Rural Engagement Officer, PC Jenkins will work with you.

"Once you've both spoken to Gilly Wimsey, and found out what she knows about Katherine, both now and from the past, look at why she moved back to the area, when she did, and who she saw. We might be wrong. Her death could have nothing to do with finding Rachael's body, and instead be linked to her return to the Cotswolds."

Inspector Evans stepped forward. "I'll oversee both investigations, of course. I'm also approving overtime for this weekend so we can make a constructive start." He looked across at Ryan and said in a sympathetic tone, "I'm sorry about the football match."

CHAPTER NINETEEN

Ryan changed into his uniform while Keya discussed her proposed plan for the afternoon with Inspector Evans.

"Ryan and I will visit Gilly and tell her about finding Kate's body. I'll ask her if she's seen Kate recently and then ask about their relationship as children and if there were any significant events."

"Shouldn't I be doing that?" asked Sergeant Unwin.

"Gilly trusts me," Keya responded. She knew Gilly didn't think highly of Sergeant Unwin as he had arrested and questioned Dotty a few months ago, which in Gilly's eyes - and those of all Dotty's friends - had shown a lack of loyalty and a lack of faith in Dotty.

"But …" began Sergeant Unwin.

"No," Inspector Evans interrupted. "Sergeant Varma is the right person to break the news to Mrs Wimsey that we've found the body of another childhood friend at Akemans. She does have her confidence."

"But …" Sergeant Unwin tried again.

"And while she's there, she may as well discover as much as she can about Mrs Wimsey's past and present relationship with the victim. Carry on, Sergeant," Inspector Evans instructed, looking up at Keya.

"And then I'll visit my village pub and see what the landlord's sister knew about Kate. It's a shame the landlord won't be back until next week."

Ryan returned wearing his uniform. As Keya turned to look at him, he asked, "Ready?"

"Yes, I think so." She turned back to Inspector Evans.

Inspector Evans nodded and instructed, "Keep me informed of anything relevant you find out, and I'll liaise with Sergeant Unwin."

Keya followed Ryan out of the room but stopped in the doorway and turned back to Inspector Evans. "Do you know how long the new extension at Akemans will be classified as a crime scene, and how much of it is?" she asked.

"I'll speak to the SOCOs on Monday morning and see what they think," replied the inspector.

In the horror of finding Kate's body, Keya hadn't considered the impact on the building project and the opening of her cafe. But it was bound to cause another delay. She just hoped it wasn't too long. Still, finding out what had happened to Kate was her priority.

Keya drove herself and Ryan to Coln Akeman. The lights were off in Dr Peter's surgery window and Keya and Ryan approached the side door of the double-fronted house.

She rang the doorbell and heard a ding-dong inside and Gilly shout, "Can someone get that?"

A smiling Dr Peter answered the door, but he froze when he saw them and drew his eyebrows together in concern as he asked in a low voice, "What's happened?"

Of course, their unannounced arrival at the weekend would worry him.

"Don't worry," blurted Keya. "It's not George, or Aunt Beanie, or any of Gilly's family."

"But someone is hurt. Is this a professional or private matter?"

"I think it better if we come inside and speak to you and Mrs Wimsey," said Ryan, formally.

"Oh dear. This is serious. Certainly, come in." Dr Peter's usual jollity was absent as he led them along the entrance hall and into the kitchen where they were met by a bright orange bottom.

Dr Peter coughed, and Gilly stood up and closed the door of the lower section of the fridge-freezer.

"Oh, sorry. I didn't realise you were there." Gilly grinned.

The kitchen, usually untidy, was even more disorganised. Gilly must have been shopping as supermarket bags were deposited on the floor, filled with items such as tinned soup, wine bottles, and liquid washing detergent.

Gilly eyed them each in turn, and her mouth fell open as she did.

"They've some bad news …" began Dr Peter, and Gilly's hand flew up to her mouth, "… but it's not your family."

"Who?" asked Gilly in a whisper.

"Her driving licence and credit cards are in the name of Katherine Dewsbury," stated Ryan.

"Katherine!" cried Gilly, stepping forward and clutching the patterned oilcloth covering the kitchen table. As the tablecloth started to move, Dr Peter grabbed a wooden chair with a wicker seat and guided his wife onto it.

"Where? Scotland? But why are you coming to tell me? Not that I don't appreciate it, but …" Gilly was starting to ramble.

"Gilly," chided Dr Peter gently, squatting down beside his wife. "Let them explain."

"I'm afraid it was closer to home. Very close," explained Keya. "Katherine's body was found at the cafe building site at Akemans."

"Really?" Dr Peter looked up at Keya. "What was she doing there?"

"That's what we'd like to know," said Ryan, before Keya had a chance to reply.

He looked across at her and muttered, "Sorry."

"No, it's all right. It's the critical question," agreed Keya. "Have you seen Katherine recently?"

"No." Gilly's eyes were wide. "Not for thirty years. I doubt if I'd know her now." She sniffed. "She was such an angelic child, with her white-blonde hair."

"So you've no idea when she returned to the Cotswolds?" asked Keya.

Gilly shook her head and moaned, "First Rachael and now Katherine."

Dr Peter straightened up and indicated with his head for Keya to follow him.

Ryan asked Gilly, "What was she like as a child?"

"Quiet, and timid, but that wasn't a surprise. Her father was very protective of her …"

Keya joined Dr Peter in the hall as he whispered, "Is Gilly in danger?"

Keya bit her lip and glanced into the kitchen.

Turning back to Dr Peter, she replied, "Honestly, I've no idea. But finding Rachael's body does seem to have unearthed, literally, something that someone wanted to stay hidden. We need to find out from Gilly if she remembers anything from the past, an event, or a person, which could be relevant to what's happening now."

Dr Peter narrowed his eyes. "That won't be easy. As Gilly said, it was over thirty years ago."

"I know," sighed Keya. "But we'll be working on this over the weekend so we can try to get to the bottom of it. If Gilly does remember anything, even a small detail, when we've left, can you let me know?"

"Of course."

"Do you have my number?"

"Somewhere, I'm sure we do." Dr Peter now looked back into the kitchen.

Keya took a card out of her wallet and handed it to him. She always carried a few with her contact details on them.

Dr Peter and Keya rejoined Gilly and Ryan in the kitchen.

"Thank you," said Gilly to Ryan, who had pulled up a chair and was sitting opposite her. "I feel better now. It's hard when someone you know dies, but a shock when it's someone from the past. I guess I imagined her living an idyllic life in a Scottish croft or seaside village. But that's like believing in fairies." Gilly looked up at Keya and asked, "But you will find out what happened to her?"

Keya smiled sadly. "Of course."

CHAPTER TWENTY

As Keya drove herself and Ryan to her home village of Ampney St Martin she said, "I'm hungry. I left without breakfast this morning. What about you?"

Ryan looked across at her and smiled. "What do you think?"

She smiled, despite the sadness of the current situation. "As long as you don't mind eating what I prepared for Kate last night, which is vegetarian, we can stop at my place for lunch, before we visit the pub."

"It sounds very healthy. But what did you think had happened to Kate when she didn't turn up?"

"I thought she'd had to work, so I wandered down to the Dog and Duck, but she wasn't there. And the lady behind the bar said she'd tried to contact Kate, but she hadn't returned her calls."

"Did SOCO give you a time of death?"

"The senior officer who examined the body estimated between six and ten last night, which is quite a window when we have to confirm suspects' alibis."

"When we have some suspects," pointed out Ryan.

"True."

Back at her little house, Ryan offered to heat up the tomato tart tatin and organise the salads, while Keya grabbed a shower and washed her hair. She felt much better when she returned to the kitchen.

Ryan tasted the couscous salad. "Delicious."

The tart tatin had crisped up nicely and was still fresh and went well with the couscous and fingers of halloumi cheese, which Keya dry-fried.

They each finished with a cake from the selection Keya had been given by the ladies of Kemble at their sale the previous day.

After lunch, they walked out of the house and were hailed by Keya's neighbour and landlady, Peggy.

"Do you think she's been waiting for us?" whispered Ryan.

Peggy peered over the boxwood hedge and said, "Nasty business at Akemans. Another body, I hear. Do you know whose?" She asked with an eager expression.

Keya wasn't sure if Peggy already knew the body's identity, but she was certainly fishing for information. Still, she had an excellent network of local friends and might be able to find out about Kate's recent history quicker than Keya could.

Keya stepped closer to the hedge and composed her face into a sorrowful but dignified expression which she used when imparting bad news. "I'm afraid it was Kate, from the Dog and Duck."

Peggy gasped. "You don't say. It'll be that Wayne she was hooked up with. Nasty piece of work."

"What can you tell me about him?" Keya asked.

"You're better off asking Coll, down at the pub."

"I would, but he's not back until next week."

"Oh no, that's not right. I saw him drive past just twenty minutes ago."

Keya glanced at Ryan. That was good news. Coll, the landlord of the Dog and Duck was bound to be able to tell them about Kate.

"Thanks, we'll go and speak to him."

"And who's your colleague?" Peggy asked in an unconvincingly innocent tone.

Ryan stepped forward and replied, "PC Ryan Jenkins, ma'am. I work with Keya at Cirencester police station."

Peggy batted her eyes and responded, "I bet you do. And let's hope we see more of you round here."

"Peggy," Keya growled.

Her neighbour gave her an impish grin and then her face contorted in pain, and she clutched at her chest.

"Are you all right?" Keya asked in a shrill voice.

Peggy closed her eyes and breathed deeply. When she opened them again, she placed a hand on top of the hedge. "The doctor said it's my heart. It's very common and nothing to worry about, but I will need a small operation. One of my arteries is blocked up."

Feeling rather guilty, but not knowing why, Keya followed Ryan onto the road and they walked down to the Dog and Duck.

They found Coll, the landlord, talking to the lady Keya had spoken to the night before. They both had podgy round faces, but the woman's was not as flushed as it had been when Keya last saw her. The bar was empty, and even Derek and his friends were absent.

"That didn't take long," sighed Coll when he saw them. "Grab a chair and I'll be over in a few minutes. I just need to finish catching up with my sis. Can I get you anything to drink?"

"We should speak to your sister as well," replied Keya. "And I'd love a cup of tea, Earl Grey, if you have some."

"Just water for me," said Ryan when Coll looked at him.

"Give us five minutes." Coll turned back to his sister.

Five minutes later, good to his word, Coll joined Keya and Ryan, who were both seated on a bench beside the wall. He placed a pint of water with ice and a lemon in it on a square beer mat in front of Ryan, and on another one, a pint of beer for himself. "Carol will join us shortly."

Carol, Coll's sister, arrived carrying a round black tray holding a teapot with cups and saucers, milk and sugar. As she poured tea for Keya and herself, Coll spoke. "Sorry business this. Good job I flew back early."

"Why was that?" asked Keya.

"Carol called and said she couldn't contact Kate."

"And I'm going to my in-laws tonight to look after my mother-in-law while my husband takes his dad out to a pub quiz. It's the only chance his dad gets to go out as his wife needs full-time care." Carol smiled sadly.

"It was no bother, anyway. I'd had enough of the sun. It was my wife who'd wanted to stay an extra week."

"What can you tell me about Kate?" asked Keya.

"She was a hard worker, and once joked she was born to the job. And she handled herself and the customers very well, don't you think, Carol?"

"Definitely, even though we were quiet this week, she was polite and attentive to everyone. She always made sure there was a vegetarian option in case you popped in late for food," said Carol, passing Keya a china cup and saucer.

That was true, thought Keya, sipping her fragrant tea. Kate had always found her something to eat.

"And she never moaned, even though I was only paying her the minimum wage," remarked Coll. "I promised I'd increase it in the summer when business picked up with the tourists, but I guess she was grateful for the job."

"Why?" asked Ryan.

Coll lowered his voice and leaned towards them, even though the pub was empty. "Her last employer wouldn't give her a reference," he revealed. "I don't know why, but I think some funny business went on."

"Do you know where she was working?" asked Keya.

"Banbury way. I'm not sure of the name of the place," replied Coll.

"I remember her mentioning Summer Lakes, or something like that," recalled Carol.

Ryan made an entry in his notebook.

"And what about her boyfriend? I understand he's not the nicest person," raised Keya.

Coll scoffed. "That's an understatement. And it certainly wouldn't surprise me if he did her in."

"And she said she had to collect some stuff from his place yesterday," added Carol. "One reason I was calling her was to check she was OK, as I was expecting her to come back to the pub with it."

"So she didn't return here after visiting him." Again, Ryan made a note. "And what's his name and address?"

Coll responded, "His name is Wayne Hourigan and I don't know his address, but you won't find him at home today, anyway."

"Why's that?" queried Ryan.

"He'll be at the footy. Cheltenham Albion are playing at home."

Ryan looked down at his notebook and muttered, "I know."

Coll chuckled. "Oh dear. Work getting in the way?"

"It is important we find out exactly what happened to Kate," said Keya, steering the conversation back to the case. "Which means we need to find Mr Hourigan."

"He'll be in no fit state to talk to tonight, but I understand he's usually in that greasy spoon cafe, next to the supermarket on the edge of Cirencester, when he pulls himself out of bed the morning after a match. I'd wait and see if he's there tomorrow, mid-morning."

Coll pulled his chin and cleared his throat before saying, "But make sure you take your colleague with you. Wayne's not the most accepting of people of colour, and especially women in positions of responsibility. Just be careful, you know what I mean."

Keya nodded. As a female Hindu police officer, she'd grown used to the strange looks she received from people, although there were less nowadays, as people in the Cotswolds had become used to her presence.

But there were still those, like the Wayne Hourigans of the world, who resented everything she stood for. And she'd never get used to some of the awful comments that were thrown at her.

Ryan looked up from his notebook and asked, "Do you know what car Kate drove?"

Keya glanced across at him. That was an excellent question.

"Yes, she had a little red mini with black stripes," answered Carol.

They would need to see if it was parked at Akemans, thought Keya.

"And can you confirm what time you last saw Kate?" Ryan's pen was poised over his notebook.

"She was out in the morning and popped back at around two. That's when she told me she was going to pick up stuff from her boyfriend's and would be back around six, ready to go out for supper …" Carol halted, looked at Keya and gasped, "With you."

CHAPTER TWENTY-ONE

A group of five young men entered the Dog and Duck pub in Ampney St Martin.

"I'll have to get back to work," said Coll, the pub landlord, as he looked up at the new arrivals.

"And I need to be off." Carol stood and placed hers and Keya's empty teacups on the black tray with the teapot and stood up.

"What next?" Ryan asked Keya.

Keya bit her lip, thinking.

"We should search Kate's room while we're here and then see if her car is at Akemans. If not, we'll need to send its description to other police stations and ask them to look out for it."

Keya and Ryan approached the bar, Ryan carrying his still half-full glass of water.

"Are you off then?" asked Coll as he pulled a pint of dark Guinness, releasing a rich aroma like a mixture of roasted barley and black coffee.

"Actually, we thought we'd take a look at Kate's room while we're here," Keya replied.

The young men in the bar were whispering to each other and shuffling their feet as they watched the exchange.

"Top of the stairs, second room on the left. It shouldn't be locked or anything." Coll placed the pint of Guinness on a bar towel and Keya watched as the dark liquid settled and separated from the creamy head.

"Coming?" asked Ryan.

Keya felt the relief of the men in the bar as she and Ryan left through the back door. They wandered past the entrance to the kitchen and found a flight of stairs at the back of the building with a clean beige carpet. Above them, they heard a vacuum cleaner.

"Coll's wife must be cleaning," remarked Ryan. "It's the first thing my mum always does when she returns from holiday."

Keya climbed the stairs. The first room on the left was a shower room and the second a small bedroom with a single bed, wardrobe, and chest of drawers. The top of the chest of drawers and the pine bedside table were cluttered with small objects. Keya started sifting through them.

Hanging out of a mother-of-pearl topped box was a Mini Cooper car key and fob.

"I'll take this," said Keya, holding it up. "Then if we do find Kate's car, we can search it."

"And move it to the station," suggested Ryan as he searched a cardboard box on the floor next to the white-painted chest of drawers.

Keya picked up a small double photo frame with a lacquered finish and two hinges so it could be safely closed. In one frame there was a picture of three smiling girls, wearing swimming costumes and eating ice cream cones.

"It's easy to spot Gilly's hair, even when she was a girl," remarked Keya, showing the photo to Ryan. "And that'll be Katherine with the very fair hair, and the dark-haired Rachael."

"Who do you think they are?" Ryan pointed to the second glass frame, which contained a length of four passport sized images.

"I remember getting photos like this taken with my sisters at one of those booths while waiting for a train. I'd guess they are Kate's parents." The young people both had long hair and were wearing horizontal-striped polo-neck jumpers. It was a style synonymous with the 1970s. "Have you found anything useful?"

"Several payslips from the pub, a copy of last year's tax return, and her V5C car logbook. There's no passport, or any personal documents like a birth certificate."

"Or wedding certificate," mused Keya.

"She wasn't married. She still used her maiden name," reasoned Ryan.

"That's not to say she didn't get married and keep her name, or get divorced and return to using it. But I think you're right. I never saw her wearing a wedding ring, and she never mentioned a husband."

Ryan had reached the back of the box and he poked his hand down and brought out several postcards.

"Anywhere nice," asked Keya as she returned to the items on the chest of drawers. "Inverness, Nairn, Cromarty. That sounds like a cross between something you'd eat and a kids' TV programme."

"Where are they?" asked Keya as she picked up a silver necklace with a dragon pendant.

Ryan checked his phone. "They're all places in the north of Scotland."

"And who are they from?" Keya held the necklace up.

"They're all signed with either a B or a D, it's difficult to tell. This one talks about people and ends with 'Please come home'." Ryan read through the other postcards as Keya opened the top drawer. She found pink and ivory lacy underwear inside.

"I think these postcards are from her dad," considered Ryan. "They talk about people and then about a mill closing down. Each of them asks, in increasing desperation, for her to return home."

"How old are they?"

"It's hard to tell. The ink on the postmarks has faded. None of them are recent though. Do you think she ran away from home?"

"It's possible," considered Keya.

"And will we have to go to Scotland to find her dad?"

Keya smiled. "Let's start by contacting the police in Inverness and see if they can track him down. I'm not sure the inspector's overtime budget will stretch to a trip to Scotland, although it would be interesting. I've never been there."

Keya and Ryan didn't find anything else they considered relevant, only clothes, toiletries, and colourful costume jewellery.

"Akemans?" asked Ryan as he climbed into Keya's police car, which she'd parked outside her house.

Derek waved to them from behind his garden gate as they drove away.

Keya was pleased to find the car park at Akemans two-thirds full, and there was even a white bus parked at the far side. If this many people were visiting in early May, then there should be plenty of trade for her cafe in the busier summer months … if she opened it in time.

"This may take a while," she considered as she climbed out of her car.

"Not necessarily," counter Ryan. "The car park would have been relatively empty when Katherine arrived, so let's start at the front. And if I keep pressing the key fob, we should see the lights flash on her car."

It was a tactic which worked and within a couple of minutes Ryan, who was taller and could see further and over even the larger vehicles, spotted Kate's red Mini in the second row, parked in front of the auction house.

Ryan opened the driver's door.

"Can you unlock the back for me?" asked Keya.

Ryan pressed the key fob and the rear boot unlocked. Keya lifted it up and found a large black suitcase and a black dustbin bag inside. She parted the top of the dustbin bag and found a handbag and, beneath it, a towel and a waterproof jacket.

"It looks like Kate collected her things from Wayne's," Keya called as she unzipped the suitcase. There was an array of clothes inside, sloppily packed, and Keya presumed Kate had been in a rush.

Ryan straightened up. "There are some magazines on the front seat, and I found this." He showed Keya a flyer for Nathan Fawcett's car show room. "He's advertising his new showroom in Cheltenham."

Keya moved round to the passenger side of the car and opened the door. She saw the magazines which were about health, fashion, or both as she popped open the glove compartment. Inside was the Mini's manual, a ten-pound note, some pound coins, and a hotel brochure.

She removed the brochure and read, "Spring Hills Hotel and Conference Centre, Banbury."

Ryan removed his notebook and consulted it. "Carol told us she thought Kate had worked at the Summer Lakes Hotel near Banbury, but do you think it was actually that one?" He pointed to the brochure Keya held.

Keya checked her watch. It was half past three. She looked across at Ryan and suggested, "One way to find out."

CHAPTER TWENTY-TWO

Ryan used his phone to navigate, and Keya drove them to the Spring Hills Hotel and Conference Centre just outside Lower Tadmarton, south-east of the Oxfordshire town of Banbury.

They drove between modern brick entrance columns and up a tarmac drive.

"There must be a golf course here," Ryan commented.

Keya glanced out of the driver's side window and spotted the fluttering red flag on top of a pole marking a hole on the golf course. There was a sandy bunker nearby. The trees on the golf course were young and small but just starting to bud.

As they approached a disappointingly modern brick building, Keya was cheered by several trees full of white or pink blossom. The entrance was in the central, double-height section of the hotel building.

"Not sure about the flags," remarked Ryan as they walked towards the front door. The sky had darkened and three flags bearing the hotel logo were cracking against their flagpoles as they were caught by strong gusts of wind.

Inside, a young woman with long dark hair and too much eye make-up greeted them. She eyed them with alarm, and glanced around the entrance foyer as they approached her.

"We didn't call you, did we?" she whispered.

A couple dressed in pale blue trousers with matching diamond patterned jumpers wandered by, eyeing Keya and Ryan suspiciously.

"Oh no," moaned the receptionist. "Mrs Cleavely isn't going to be happy about this."

"And who is she?" asked Keya.

"The manager."

Keya looked at Ryan before she said, "Then we'd better start with her. Where will we find her?"

"Oh. She's busy today. She only sees people by appointment."

Keya looked around as two smartly dressed women entered the hotel and, seeing her, turned and walked back out.

"Then we'll have to wait here until she makes that appointment."

The receptionist flinched and grabbed a phone on her desk. Covering the mouthpiece, Keya still heard her whisper. "Two police officers are in reception, and they're worrying the guests."

She put the phone down and said, "Take that corridor," she pointed to her left, "and Mrs Cleavely will meet you."

Keya didn't catch what the receptionist said to herself as they walked towards the corridor entrance, but she didn't think it was something the guests would have wanted to hear.

A middle-aged woman wearing a plain navy-blue dress and matching jacket barred their progress along the corridor.

"It's obvious who you are," she remarked acidly and led them into a spacious and beautifully decorated room. She did not suggest they sit on the plush light blue sofas beside the fireplace, but instead they all remained standing.

"What is the problem, officers?"

"No problem," replied Keya in a polite, calm tone. "We're following up some enquires and looking into the history of a woman called Katherine Dewsbury."

The woman folded her arms and raised her eyebrows. "Landed herself in trouble, has she? Well that's not a surprise."

"So you do know her? Did she work here?" Keya glanced round the opulent room.

"Yes, for about nine months. She was actually excellent with the guests, it was just …" Mrs Cleavely didn't finish her sentence.

Keya returned her attention to Mrs Cleavely. "Would you mind telling us why she left?"

Mrs Cleavely snapped, "Yes, I would mind." She took a deep breath as she tried to control herself.

Keya's tone was frosty as she replied, "Katherine Dewsbury died under suspicious circumstances. So it's our duty to ask awkward and even uncomfortable questions, either here or at Cirencester police station, if you'd prefer."

Mrs Cleavely remained rigid, but a pulse in her neck throbbed and her face had grown paler as she muttered, "You need to speak to my husband."

Keya waited for her to elaborate.

"You'll find him in the fitness centre, making sure our female guests have everything they need." Mrs Cleavely's tone was bitter.

"Thank you," said Keya politely as she and Ryan left the office and returned to reception.

An American couple speaking to the receptionist stepped back in surprise as Keya and Ryan approached.

"Where can we find the fitness centre?" asked Keya.

For an answer, the wide-eyed receptionist pointed towards the opposite corridor.

The corridor took them past the large restaurant, which was light and airy with windows looking out over the golf course.

They left the main building and followed a gravel path between well-maintained flower beds with several delicate flowers between those which looked as if they'd bloom later in the season. Keya felt a drop of rain.

The hotel's fitness centre was a single-storey building with white walls and timber panels. They passed through the entrance lobby, with signs for male and female changing rooms, and into a bright, airy gym.

One end consisted of a glass wall looking out over another section of the golf course and a lake. Rain drops splattered against it.

A man with short hair wearing gym clothes with a small grey towel hanging round his neck was leaning over a lady lying in a contraption which Keya presumed was used to increase leg strength. He adjusted a pin in a stack of metal weights and stood up as the lady pushed at a metal plate.

"Good job," he said, placing his hand on her thigh. "Five more reps at that weight."

The lady glanced across at Ryan and Keya, and her eyes widened. The man turned round to see what had caught her attention and for a moment, Keya thought he was about to run. But he composed his face into a relaxed expression and sauntered towards them.

"Officers, I hope our guests haven't been disturbing the peace."

"Are you Mr Cleavely?"

"Neil, please. Mr Cleavely sounds very formal." The man tried to sound relaxed, but his forehead was glistening with sweat, and Keya didn't think it was from an earlier workout.

"Mr Cleavely," repeated Keya, "we'd like to speak to you about Katherine Dewsbury."

Mr Cleavely's eyes darted from Keya to Ryan, and she felt Ryan tense.

"Katherine, lovely girl," joked Mr Cleavely.

When neither Keya nor Ryan spoke, he added, "Why don't you come to my office?"

He led them to a small room at the side of the gym, which was the opposite of his wife's office. It was cramped and untidy, with brown cardboard boxes bearing the names of what looked like nutrition companies stacked on top of each other.

Shelves at the back contained a variety of round plastic containers. But, like his wife, he didn't ask them to sit.

His tone was less genial when he asked, "What's Kate been saying?"

"Why would she say anything?" responded Keya, narrowing her eyes.

Ryan asked, "Were you having an affair with her?"

Keya thought she saw relief in Mr Cleavely's eyes, and his shoulders relaxed as he turned to Ryan and, smiling once again, said, "She's a beautiful woman, and my wife doesn't have much time for me."

"But she found out about the affair?" Ryan pressed.

"She did."

"And that's the reason Katherine left?"

"My wife told her to leave and refused to give her a reference. Kate kicked up a fuss, of course, but there wasn't much she could do. I heard she found work in a village pub. Don't tell me she had an affair with the landlord."

Keya answered, "No, she didn't, but her body was found this morning and we're questioning all those who'd known her and had a reason to harm her." Keya watched Mr Cleavely closely.

He tried to hide his reaction, but Keya noted his hands tighten as he flinched. He was afraid. He was hiding something. But she didn't think they'd find out what it was today. Still she asked, "When did you last see Kate?"

Again, Mr Cleavely appeared relieved as he relaxed his hands. "Not since she left here just before Christmas."

"And have you spoken or corresponded with her in any way?"

Mr Cleavely widened his stance. "I haven't had any contact with her since she left. And now, I need to get back to my guests."

She was right. They wouldn't get any more out of Mr Cleavely today.

She and Ryan walked back the way they'd come and smiled at the relieved looking receptionist as they left.

"Back to the station?" asked Ryan as they rushed to their car through the driving rain.

"Yes, I'll drop you back and we can update the inspector."

Ryan turned on the radio and for the hour's drive back to Cirencester, he listened to the second half of Cheltenham Albion's football match while Keya concentrated on the road, peering through the windscreen and driving rain.

The match ended as Keya drove into Cirencester town centre and the rain eased.

"I suppose I didn't miss much," moaned Ryan. "To give away a penalty in the eighty-eighth minute."

"But they were one goal down anyway," consoled Keya.

"They still had time to score an equaliser, but not after that penalty."

Keya parked, and they stepped round puddles as they entered the police station. The reception was full, and Ryan had to intervene as two young men dressed in tweed jackets squared up to each other.

"You can bring that one with you," said a relieved desk sergeant.

Ryan propelled one of the men, who struggled in vain, through the door into the main police station.

"Put him in interview room two," said the desk sergeant. "No wonder Stan Rowbottom took early retirement. I'm not sure how he lasted so long dealing with the likes of this lot."

Keya entered her team's room and found Sergeant Unwin surrounded by paperwork. "Busy afternoon?" she asked.

"It's amazing the way officers handled themselves thirty years ago. We couldn't get away with such techniques now, which makes me question some of the statements that were made. And I can't find anything about the fifth guest staying at the pub. Only a note that he was house hunting, but where and what his appointments were, I've no idea."

"I wondered about that, too," said Ryan, entering the room and straightening his jacket.

Sergeant Unwin looked at him and asked, "What happened to you?"

"An agricultural college student was a bit worse for wear and tried to take a swing at me but overbalanced and fell on the floor."

Keya wondered if that was really what had happened, but she didn't press. Instead, she asked, "Is the inspector in?"

"Yes, he's been on the phone with SOCO most of the afternoon. They refused to set up a tent, so this rain will have washed any remaining evidence away."

"Oh," said Keya, halting. If the areas where the bodies had been found were no longer of use forensically, the builders might be able to continue their work.

The door opened and Inspector Evans stepped out. He'd removed his tie and undone the top button of his cream shirt.

"That's that," he muttered and then looked at Keya. "You can tell your builders to start again on Monday. This rain's ruined the crime scenes."

Keya couldn't help smiling as she replied, "Thank you."

"So while Sergeant Unwin has been busy here, what have you two found out?" asked the inspector.

Between them, Keya and Ryan ran through their interviews with Gilly and Neil Cleavely.

"You think Neil Cleavely is a suspect, and he wasn't telling you everything about his relationship with Katherine?" queried the inspector.

"I do," replied Keya.

"Then what's your plan of action for tomorrow?"

"Breakfast at a greasy spoon."

Ryan's eyes brightened.

"To find and interview Kate's boyfriend. I'm taking my pub landlord's advice and meeting him on neutral ground with Ryan. But as Kate had already collected her stuff from him, I'm not sure he's our man."

"Speak to him anyway," directed the inspector.

"And then I'll drop Ryan at Akemans, and he can drive Kate's car back here."

"If I can fit in it," grinned Ryan.

"Then look into Neil Cleavely. Follow your gut on that one," suggested Inspector Evans.

"Sergeant," the inspector turned to Nick. "Do you want Ryan to help find the missing pub guest tomorrow?"

"That would be useful," agreed Nick.

"Good work everyone. Time to go home," said the inspector, yawning. "And PC Jenkins."

"Yes, sir."

"Sorry about the football score."

CHAPTER TWENTY-THREE

Keya drove home, looking forward to a lazy evening on the sofa watching TV. She didn't often feel like watching it but today she was tired and as she was working again tomorrow …

Her phone rang, interrupting her thoughts. She groaned. It was her sister, Zivah.

"Hi sis." She tried to sound happy to hear from her.

"I'm just calling to make sure you haven't forgotten about this evening's dinner."

Keya didn't answer. She had forgotten.

"Keya?"

"Yes, I'm still here."

"Aadi's bringing his parents to supper and Mum wants us all there. No exceptions."

"OK. OK. I'm just heading home. Give me a chance to shower and change."

"And wear something … feminine. No jeans. OK?"

"I hear you, sis. See you later."

In truth, she was relieved Zivah had called as she was already in her mother's bad books and missing tonight's dinner would have led to a huge row about selfishness, and family values, and who knew what else. Her mother was desperate to impress her sister's future in-laws.

Keya drove to her parent's home on the outskirts of Gloucester. When she was younger, they'd lived above the shop her parents ran in a not particularly pleasant part of the city. But her father had attended night school and learned about bookkeeping.

He started work at a local furniture store, doing their books, but when other members of the Hindu community heard about his new job, they asked him to complete their accounts and deal with the British tax authorities.

Slowly, her father had built up his business, working above the shop and visiting his clients at their premises. When he'd saved enough, he sold the lease on the shop and their flat above it and moved the family to a new housing estate, while he took a small office in a nearby business park.

Keya remembered her mother's delight when they'd first visited their new home. She'd run her hand along the laminate kitchen worktop and admired the shiny stainless steel sink. Keya had been more excited about upstairs, as she and her brother were both given their own rooms.

Hers was tiny, and she could only fit in a bed and a desk. But she didn't mind. It was her space and she no longer had to share with her two sisters.

Her parents still lived in the same house, even though many of the estate's original occupants had moved to larger and shinier new estates built further out of Gloucester.

And while many of the houses looked dated and stained, and their occupants neglected their outside spaces, her mother had maintained her immaculate garden.

Of her siblings, Keya was the only one who had moved out, to the delight of her youngest sister, Maitri, who'd immediately moved into her room.

Keya noticed the new white Honda Civic parked in the drive as she pulled in to the curb, just beyond the entrance to her parent's house.

Aadi and his parents must have arrived already.

She stepped out of her car and straightened her brown tunic top, printed with silver motifs. She was wearing tight plain brown pashmina trousers with it, and a pair of delicate gold sandals. The top strap of the left one was biting into her foot after driving.

She let herself into the house and found her mother, as usual, in the kitchen. "You're late," hissed her mother as she eyed Keya. "But you look beautiful." She stepped forward and hugged her daughter. "Now make yourself useful and hand these around."

Keya was used to acting as a waitress when her parents entertained and actually preferred it to having to speak to the guests. She carried a platter of vegetable samosas through to the living room. Like many families, her parents had built a conservatory style extension which increased the size of the room, and brought in more light, but it became unbearably hot in summer.

"And this, as you know, is my oldest daughter, Keya," said her father, who was speaking to Aadi's parents.

Keya approached them, offering her platter of samosas as she whispered to her father, "Sorry I'm late. I had to work today."

"Your sister thought you'd forgotten." Her father raised his eyebrows, and she bit her lip, and felt her cheeks flush.

"Zivah told us you work in the police station in Cirencester. A clerk or something."

Keya could see her sister grimacing and shaking her head, but Keya stood a little taller and replied, "I'm officially the Rural Engagement Officer, but I also work with one of the serious crime teams. Today we've been investigating the deaths of a woman and a young girl."

"Oh dear," muttered Aadi's mum, stepping back.

Aadi's father dropped the samosa he'd just lifted from her tray.

Zivah rushed forward and said, "Don't worry. I'll clear it up. Keya, why don't you offer Aadi one of those?"

Keya left her father and his guests and made her way across to Aadi, who was now standing by himself. He chuckled, "Do you always get that reaction when you tell people what you do?"

"Within the Hindu community, yes. I'm not sure why everyone is so shocked that a Hindu woman can be a police officer."

"You know exactly why," Aadi retorted, picking up a samosa. "But do you enjoy it?"

"I do, although certain recent events made me reconsider if I was doing the right thing. But I think I'm on track now. I'm not working full-time anymore, and my work is mostly with the rural communities."

"Zivah tells me you're opening a cafe."

"I hope so, as long as we don't find any more dead bodies."

Aadi choked on his samosa and reached for his glass of water. After taking a sip and emptying his mouth, he asked, "What bodies?"

Keya told him about their current case.

"I know Nathan Fawcett," said Aadi. "He's searching for a site for another showroom on the edge of Gloucester, and I think he's interested in one owned by the company I work for."

"Wow, that will be his third showroom. His business must be doing really well."

Keya's mother entered the room and whispered to her father, who announced, "Dinner is served."

CHAPTER TWENTY-FOUR

On Sunday morning Keya walked out of her bathroom and heard her phone ringing. With her towel wrapped around her she reached over to her bedside table and picked up her phone.

"Morning, Keya," said a bright-sounding Ryan. "Mum'll give me a lift to the cafe this morning as she's going to the supermarket to do her shopping. Are we still meeting at 10?"

Keya glanced at the LED display on her digital alarm clock. "Let's say a quarter to."

"No problem. See you later."

Keya dressed in jeans and a casual top. She'd agreed with Inspector Evans that if Wayne Hourigan saw her and Ryan in the cafe in their police uniform, he might make a run for it. They both had spare uniforms at the station, should they need them later.

It was just after a quarter to ten when she turned off the roundabout on the edge of Cirencester. Joe's Diner was in front of her and she was surprised it was still in business as a McDonalds had recently been built behind it.

She parked and entered the cafe. Half a dozen tables were occupied. Every table was the same, with a beige Formica top and four moulded red plastic chairs, on steel frames bolted to the floor.

There was no chance of moving them, or anyone using them as

weapons, which was probably the intention of the original owner, who she presumed was Joe, when he had them put in.

Ryan was seated by a window reading a large two-sided laminated menu.

"Hiya," greeted Keya as she sat down.

Ryan moved the menu to one side and said, "What a great way to start a Sunday. Just a shame we'll have to spoil it with an interview."

"Do we actually know what our suspect looks like?" asked Keya.

"Ah," grinned Ryan. "I spoke to the guy behind the counter, John, who's the son of the original owner, Joe. He knows Wayne. A regular customer, it seems, and he said he'd give me the heads up, although he isn't expecting him until closer to ten thirty." Ryan moved the menu back in front of his face. "So I thought we could order breakfast."

Keya picked up a second menu. There was a full English vegetarian option, but her attention was caught by American-style pancakes with berries and mascarpone cream.

"Will we be able to claim this since we're on a stakeout?" queried Ryan from behind his menu.

He sounded excited and Keya smiled to herself at his enthusiasm. She said, "I'll pay and then discuss it with the inspector. Do we wait for someone to come over or order at the counter?"

Ryan lowered his menu. "Order at the counter. Can I have a full English breakfast with two fried eggs and white toast? And a latte."

Keya raised her eyebrows as she pushed herself off the plastic chair and strode over to the counter.

"You two together?" asked the man behind the counter, who Keya presumed was John.

"Yes, and can I order breakfast?"

"Certainly." John picked up a small pad of white paper and a pencil. Kaya repeated Ryan's order and added the American pancakes for herself and an English Breakfast tea. Earl Grey was too floral for this morning.

John totted up the prices and calculated, "Twenty pounds exactly."

Keya handed over two £10 notes and asked, "Can I have a receipt?"

"I'll bring it over with your drinks." John turned and handed the slip to someone through a hatch in the wall behind him.

"How is it living back with your parents?" Keya asked Ryan as she sat down.

"It's nice being cooked for, and I actually help Mum and make some suppers, but she does fuss over me. And I prefer to do my own washing now."

Ryan had been living with two friends, but one of them had found a girlfriend who spent more and more time in their small house until they found she was living with them. Rows had started as she'd refused to pull her weight with household chores or pay her fair share. The other friend was sent to Wales for a six month project, so Ryan had also made the decision to move out and return to his parents.

"Will you look for somewhere else?"

"Maybe, but I'd prefer to be on my own, which either means a tiny bedsit or somewhere expensive."

Keya nodded in understanding. If she had to leave her little house, she wouldn't find anything nearly as nice for the rent she was paying.

John placed two plain white mugs on the table and a handwritten receipt in front of Keya. "Breakfast won't be too long, and I expect Wayne will be here soon. But let him drink some coffee before you approach him."

John left and Ryan picked up a thin white packet of sugar, but he didn't open it. "When do you think Dotty will be back?" he asked.

Keya narrowed her eyes. "Why? Are you thinking of moving into her cottage?"

"I was wondering about it. I could pay her rent, so she didn't have to, and help Norman and Aunt Beanie. I like the set-up. Company when you want it, but also your own space."

Keya sipped her tea before replying, "That's not a bad idea, actually. You should email or message her and suggest it."

John arrived with their breakfast. A large oval plate for Ryan ladened with two fried eggs, two sausages, a slice of black pudding, two hash browns, roasted mushrooms and tomatoes, and a pool of baked beans.

Keya wondered how he would eat it all, but as she looked down at the stack of pancakes on her own plate, she wondered the same thing. Strawberries, blackberries, raspberries, blueberries, and redcurrants were piled on top and cascaded down the sides. And between the pancakes, there were layers of rich mascarpone cheese.

Jim returned with Ryan's toast and whispered, "Wayne's just parking that beast of a car of his."

Ryan and Keya looked out of the window as a scruffy man wearing a red checked shirt and ripped jeans climbed out of a large red double-cab pickup.

"But eat your breakfast before it gets cold," instructed John.

Distractedly, Keya cut into her pancake stack while trying not to look out of the window.

Ryan attacked his breakfast with gusto.

Keya was aware of the cafe door opening but resisted the temptation to look round.

Ryan glanced up, registered something, and returned his attention to his plate.

"He's taking a seat by the opposite wall," whispered Ryan, cutting the end off a fat sausage.

"As John suggested, let's give him time to settle while we eat our breakfast."

Keya began to feel defeated halfway through her stack of pancakes. She gathered the remaining berries and some of the mascarpone and ate them with bite-size pieces of pancake.

Finishing, she placed her knife and fork together and sat back, feeling full. "That was tasty, but I can't eat another mouthful."

Ryan was making unwavering progress through his breakfast.

As Keya picked up her mug of tea, Ryan muttered, "John's just taken our suspect his coffee."

"OK, we'll give him a couple more minutes,"

Ryan concentrated on eating the remaining egg, bacon, and sausage on his plate. He placed his knife and fork on either side of it, indicating that he wasn't finished, and wiped his hands on a white paper napkin from a wooden box on the table.

"I'll go and stand by the door in case he tries to make a run for it. Give me a minute."

Ryan picked up his notepad and moved towards the door.

Keya placed her mug on the table, took a deep breath, and stood up. She approached Wayne, who was sitting alone at a table for four.

Out of the corner of her eye, she saw Ryan step back from the door and allow a family with two young children to enter. They saw Wayne and moved across to take a table near Keya and Ryan's.

"Mr Hourigan," said Keya as she stood beside his table, next to the red plastic chair positioned opposite him.

"Who wants to know?"

Keya removed her black warrant card holder from her pocket and, like the TV shows, opened it for Wayne to see.

"I'm Sergeant Varma from Gloucestershire Police."

"What do you want with me?" asked Wayne as he looked around. He glanced back at the door and met Ryan's serious expression. "I see you've brought reinforcements."

"Like you, we thought we'd start with a hearty breakfast before continuing our work on Katherine Dewsbury's case."

"Kate?" Wayne's eyes narrowed. "What's she done?"

"I'm afraid she's got herself killed."

"No way. Hey. You're not trying to pin this on me, are you?" The volume and pitch of Wayne's voice rose. He once again glanced back at Ryan.

"All we want to do is ask you a few questions about Kate, when you last saw her, who her friends were, and any arguments or disagreement that you know about. That sort of thing. For instance, we know she collected her stuff from you on Friday afternoon."

"Yeah, but I was out at work, so I didn't see her."

"And where do you work?"

"I'm a mechanic at a place on the Burford Road. Look, why don't you take a seat? I don't like the police, but I do want to know what happened to Kate, and if anyone else is involved, who they are."

Keya slid onto the chair opposite Wayne. She wasn't sure if that was a cue, but a moment later John carried over a plate of breakfast identical to the one Ryan had ordered.

Ryan approached and asked, "Everything OK?"

Keya nodded.

Ryan glanced back at the remains of his breakfast. "Do you mind?"

"Feel free," replied Wayne, cutting into a runny fried egg.

Keya shuffled over to the second seat as John placed a fresh mug of tea in front of her. "I thought you might need this."

"Thanks," she smiled at him gratefully.

As Ryan settled and restarted his breakfast, Wayne remarked, "I'm not always as bad as people make out. I know I have a temper, especially after a few drinks, and I did turn it on Kate. I'm really sorry about that as she was a great lass and too good for me. I wish I could have kept hold of her. Perhaps I could have stopped whichever b…"

Ryan coughed.

"… did it in for her. What happened?" asked Wayne.

Keya knew the discovery of a body in the trench was already public news, so she told Wayne about it.

Wayne looked thoughtful as he spooned baked beans into his mouth. Some tomato juice dribbled onto his chin, which he seemed unaware of. Keya tried but failed to ignore it. "You've got … just there." She touched her own chin.

Wayne removed a napkin from an identical wooden box to the one on their table and dabbed his chin. "Thanks." He continued, "She did mention Akemans a few times. Usually at night after a couple of glasses of wine. She seemed to be reminiscing about old times. A better life. Do you think she just went for a visit and fell into the hole?"

"It's possible," conceded Keya.

"I've no idea who would want to harm her, although I know folk will be blaming it on me, so you make it clear," Wayne stabbed his knife in her direction, "that I had nothing to do with it."

"We'll need to check your alibi for Friday evening," said Keya.

"Sure. I left work at half five and headed for a pint at the Golden Miller on the Burford Road with a few lads from work. I met some more mates and didn't leave till gone ten. Someone gave me a lift to the end of my road, and I grabbed fish and chips and walked home. In truth, I didn't want to be around when Kate collected her stuff. I was ashamed of my behaviour and worried about what I might do if I saw her. I can be a real idiot."

This morose man in front of her was not the person Keya had been expecting.

"I'm forty this year, and what do I have to show for my life? A string of jobs at one garage and then another and no wife or family. I don't own my house. I don't really own anything."

"Then why not travel?" suggested Ryan as he ate his last mushroom.

"Me? I've hardly been out of Gloucestershire. I did visit London once, but I got lost and didn't go back."

"A mechanic is a very sought after skill. I'm sure there are loads of places abroad where you could work, even if it's for a charity and all you get is your food and lodging," explained Ryan.

"And some beer money," said Wayne dreamily.

Was the clean cut, fresh-faced Ryan really giving this scruffy, bad tempered middle-aged man career advice? Keya shook her head.

"Well, you're not going anywhere until we've cleared up this case. We'll visit the pub and check your alibi, and also your work, to check what time you left. Where is that?"

"Fawcett's showroom."

"You work for Nathan Fawcett?" asked Keya, somewhat surprised.

"Yeah, but he won't vouch for me. He hardly speaks to me except to instruct me to check or clean a car. Besides, he wasn't around Friday. Probably looking for more sites to expand his business empire."

CHAPTER TWENTY-FIVE

John refused Keya's offer to pay for her second cup of tea and she and Ryan left, but not until Ryan had agreed to meet up with Wayne and discuss his work and life options.

As they stepped outside, Keya asked, "Do you offer help to every middle-aged man you meet who's lost his way?"

"Sometimes," Ryan said. "I saw my uncle spiral out of control when his wife left him and, not knowing what to do, found himself involved with a gang of thieves. He landed himself in jail for five years."

"Does the inspector know about this?" Keya knew the police force wasn't always happy about its employees having family members who broke the law.

"Sure, he said it gave me a human touch and enables me to see that not everything is black and white. But I try to show similar men that there is another way and so many opportunities if they'll just have the courage to take them."

"Good luck with Wayne," offered Keya, thinking Ryan was wasting his time. "OK, next we'll go to Akemans to collect Kate's car."

Keya drove. It was a bright pleasant day and when she'd watched Ryan drive out of Akemans in Kate's Mini, she decided to have a walk before returning to the office. The building site was padlocked shut.

There was no crime scene tape beside the foundations for the cafe extension and the piece she and Brad had put up near the waterwheel had snapped and the longer end snaked across the ground from the post it was attached to beside the river.

Keya followed the metal fencing down to the bank of the River Coln and walked along it for a minute before stopping and watching the water flow gently by, carrying twigs and branches presumably broken off during the previous afternoon's storm.

She tipped her head back and soaked in gentle rays of sunshine.

All was peaceful until she heard sniggering and a boy's voice whisper, "Do you think she's seen us?"

Keya opened her eyes but didn't move her head. She felt rather than heard movement near her and suddenly she turned and faced two boys of about ten, who were manoeuvring themselves around the edge of the metal fence panel beside the river.

"Uh-oh!" shouted one of the boys as he pulled himself round and ran up the line of fencing. His friend followed, but his jacket snagged on the fence. He yanked himself free and scampered after his mate.

Keya let them go. After all the rain, there was little damage they could have done, even though she suspected they'd dared themselves to visit the waterwheel channel because a skeleton had been found there.

When she reached the fencing panel, she removed the torn piece of blue jacket left by the boy. It was caught on a hook designed for attaching another panel to the fence. She hadn't meant to scare the boys, and she hoped the one who'd torn his jacket wouldn't be in too much trouble with his mum.

She stopped as she noticed a second piece of fabric caught on the hook. It was bright yellow, like the vests and jackets worn by the builders working on the site. It must have come from whoever erected the fence.

Glancing down at the ground, she noticed it was covered with many different footprints. Clearly the boys were not the first people to enter the building site at this point.

Keya returned to the car park but before she climbed into her car, she sent a message to Vic Peters telling him the police had finished and he and his men could continue with the extension on Monday.

She didn't send Rowan a message as she wanted to speak to him in person and pin him down to a date to continue with the removal of the waterwheel. She'd call him first thing on Monday.

Then she got into her car and drove to the police station.

When she arrived in her team's office, Ryan and Nick were combing through pieces of paper. "The trouble is," said Nick, "we don't know which houses were for sale, and what budget our mystery man had."

"But we could find out what estate agents were operating in Cirencester at the time," suggested Ryan. "Not all of them will have survived, as house buyers have moved to the internet, but if he was going high-end, then he might have tried Knight Frank on Cricklade Street."

"Sergeant!" called Inspector Evans from his open door. He was also in casual clothes, having exchanged his brown suit for brown trousers and a fawn polo shirt.

Keya entered his office and stood in front of his desk as she recounted the meeting she and Ryan had had with Wayne.

"That sounds disappointingly civil," remarked the inspector dryly when she finished. "Although I'm not saying he isn't our killer. Follow up his alibi at the car showroom and then the pub which," he glanced at his watch, "should open soon. Then take the rest of the afternoon off. There's not much more you can do until we speak to the SOCOs on Monday morning. And I made it clear to them yesterday that we do need answers first thing."

"Thank you, Inspector," replied Keya gratefully. She bit her lip before asking, "And about breakfast?"

"Yes, you can submit it to expenses. I don't mind supporting Joe and John. I know they've struggled to keep going with that other fast-food restaurant opening up near them."

Keya drove to the Burford Road and pulled into the forecourt of Nathan Fawcett's car showroom. As she weaved between cars to get to the service area of the main building, she saw Nathan clap a bald-headed man on the back. Clearly Nathan was in full sales mode.

The service area was quiet. Should she come back tomorrow? A bearded man walked out of a door to her left, holding an oil-streaked mug and asked, "Can I help you?"

As she was in plain clothes, Keya once again showed her warrant card as she said, "What time did Wayne Hourigan leave on Friday?"

"Five thirty, with the rest of us. We headed down to the Golden Miller for a pint. I just stayed for one, but Wayne and some of the other lads looked settled in for the evening. I couldn't tell you what time he left. Is this about his ex, Kate? Was she the one found at the auction house?"

"I'm afraid so," confirmed Keya.

"That's sad, that is. Wayne's rough around the edges, and I'm not saying he wouldn't raise his hand to a lass when he'd had a few drinks, but there's no way he'd have wanted Kate dead. He was desperate to win her back."

Keya left the service area, returned to her car, and drove half a mile down the Burford Road, towards Cirencester, before turning in and parking behind the Golden Miller pub.

It didn't look like somewhere she'd enjoy visiting and she was pleased it was Sunday lunchtime and, hopefully, too early for most of the regulars.

She was right. The main room was empty, although a couple of men were playing pool in another room.

"What can I get you?" asked a middle-aged, bored sounding woman behind the bar. For the third time that day, Keya showed her warrant card and asked, "Did you see Wayne Hourigan here on Friday evening?"

"Sure, he and his workmates arrived just after half past five, which they usually do, and, as usual, Wayne didn't leave until gone ten. I'm not sure he wouldn't have stayed until closing time except a friend offered him a lift home. Is this about his ex, Kate? You don't suspect Wayne of anything, do you?"

Had everyone heard about Kate's body being found?

"We're just following up enquires and establishing alibis."

"Well I'll tell you this for free. Wayne was in no state to swing a stick without falling over when he left here on Friday night. I'm always surprised he makes it home at all, but he must have some inner self-preservation which always gets him there. He's not your man."

As she left the pub, Keya was thinking the same thing. So where would the investigation take her on Monday?

CHAPTER TWENTY-SIX

Keya arrived at Cirencester Police station feeling bright and alert on Monday morning. She had left the Golden Miller pub the previous day and gone straight home.

After such a large breakfast at Joe's Cafe, she hadn't needed lunch, so she'd been able to clean the house and sort out her washing before she felt the need for a rest.

And watching Sunday evening TV was probably more relaxing than the game shows shown on a Saturday night. She thought of Dotty as she watched an antique show filmed at a large country house in Norfolk.

Inspector Evans arrived soon after her. "I'm glad you're here. SOCO needs to speak to us urgently and they want to do so via video call. I have no idea how and as I told Ryan to have a lie-in, I don't expect to see him until mid-morning."

Inspector Evans opened his office door and turned on the lights. He manoeuvred around his desk and switched his computer on.

"Would you like a cup of tea, sir?" Keya asked, hovering in the doorway.

The inspector stabbed the keyboard with a fleshy finger. "You sort this out, Sergeant, and I'll make the tea."

Keya settled herself at the inspector's desk. There was a

photograph of his elderly but formidable mum, and one of a rugby team with a large hill in the background. Probably in Wales.

The desk was messy, and she moved a haphazard pile of papers to one side and pulled the keyboard and mouse towards her as she clicked on the link for the online call with SOCO.

An earnest-looking man with black glasses and short dark hair appeared on the screen. "You're not Inspector Evans."

"No, I'm just setting the meeting up for him," replied Keya.

Inspector Evans entered and pushed a report to one side so he could place a grey and white striped mug on a coaster which was decorated with a red dragon on a green and white background.

Keya stood up, and the inspector passed her a mug with 'I love mornings' on it. The love was a large yellow heart.

"Pull up a pew," instructed the inspector as he sat down, but Keya remained standing behind him.

"Sebastian, I'm impressed. I said first thing Monday morning, but I didn't expect to hear from you before I'd had a chance to drink my first cup of tea."

"This is important. I almost called you yesterday afternoon, but I didn't want to disturb you."

"You wouldn't have. My team's been busy all weekend. Didn't want the trail going cold. So what is so important?" asked Inspector Evans.

"We've muddled up the identities of the bodies."

Keya wrinkled her forehead. What could he mean?

"I don't understand," replied the inspector, as he paused, the mug raised to his mouth.

"We were finally able to isolate readable DNA from the skeleton, but when the results came back, we thought it had been muddled with that from the body found in the trench. So I personally ran DNA tests yesterday morning on both the skeleton of the girl and the body of the woman and they are not who we thought they were. The young girl, who died between thirty and thirty-five years ago, was Katherine Dewsbury ..."

"What?!" cried Keya in confusion. Hot tea sloshed out of her cup and onto Inspector Evans' shoulder.

"Sergeant," he growled.

"Sorry, sir. It's such a shock," stammered Keya. "Let me grab some tissues," she garbled.

"Later," commanded the inspector in a voice which she knew left no room for arguing. "Go on, Sebastian."

"I thought that would surprise you. It certainly confused us. Especially as the DNA of the woman found on Saturday morning matches the DNA from the original missing person case for Rachael Fawcett."

Inspector Evans removed a stained white handkerchief from his suit jacket pocket and dabbed at his shoulder as he asked slowly and deliberately, "Are you telling me, that Katherine Dewsbury died when she was a child, and Rachael Fawcett, for some reason, assumed her identity and has been living as Katherine all these years?"

"I cannot tell you who Rachael has been pretending to be, only that she died between half past four and half past six on Friday evening."

The timing of Kate's death had changed. Keya realised that meant Wayne Hourigan could have killed her, and then returned to work and gone to the pub with his colleagues. She needed to check if anyone had seen him at work between four and leaving for the pub at half past five.

Inspector Evans picked up a pen and clicked the end on the table so the ball point extended and retracted.

"We are presuming that DNA was Rachael's," considered the inspector.

"It's what was in the file. But I am certain the young girl was Katherine. For some reason, her mother's DNA was in the system file, and it's a familial match."

The inspector stopped his annoying antics with his pen. "Do you know what weapon was used to kill Katherine, no, Rachael, on Friday?"

"It was definitely blunt force trauma. She was struck on the front of the head, above her left eye, but from the damage to the skull, we can't identify the exact weapon."

The inspector's shoulders sagged.

"Sorry to be the bearer of such bad news this morning, Inspector." Sebastian removed his glasses and ran a hand through his hair.

"Better we know now rather than waste any more police time," muttered the inspector.

"Excuse me," said Keya quietly.

"Speak up if you have something to say, Sergeant," directed the inspector.

After the tea incident, Keya hadn't wanted to interrupt the two senior men.

"Did the young girl die from the same wound?"

"Good question." Sebastian reached for something out of sight, and she saw him open a brown paper file. "I haven't worked on the body directly, but the report states she also died from a blow to the head, although from the damage to the skull, I'd say the weapon had a smaller impact point and was used with greater force than that on the older woman."

"Are you saying that the person who killed … I'm getting confused … the woman, didn't need to be that strong? Another woman, for instance?" asked the inspector.

Sebastian drew his eyes together. "I've encountered women capable of supreme acts of strength, but to answer your question, the strength needed to cause such wounds depends on the weapon used. Something with a small impact area like a hammer would need more force than say a spade, with a much larger impact area."

"I'm not sure that helps,' grunted the inspector.

"But would the person who killed Kate on Friday have been standing close to her?" asked Keya. "Sorry, but I knew her as Kate, and to start calling her Rachael will only confuse me and the other people who knew her by that name."

Sebastian drew his lips together. "In answer to your question, I'd say yes, reasonably close. Close enough to have a conversation."

"Or argument," muttered the inspector.

"I still can't understand why Kate was at the building site," pondered Keya.

"That's for you to find out, Sergeant," retorted the inspector.

On the screen, Sebastian consulted his watch. "I have a staff meeting. I'll email you the report before I go. And I should be free from ten thirty if you have any more questions."

"Thank you," said the inspector and Sebastian's face disappeared from the computer monitor.

Keya was still staring at it when Inspector Evans asked, "So what do you think of that, Sergeant?"

Keya sipped the remains of her tea and then muttered, "It turns everything on its head."

CHAPTER TWENTY-SEVEN

Keya returned to her desk and spotted the note she'd left to remind herself to call Rowan about restarting renovation work on the waterwheel.

Although her mind was still processing the information Sebastian had given them, and the change in the identities of the bodies, she needed to call Rowan.

"Hey there, how you doing? Any more bodies turn up?" Rowan drawled.

Keya ignored the question. She needed Rowan to focus on the waterwheel and not find another excuse to delay his work. "The police have released the site so you can remove the waterwheel."

"Let me see …"

"Rowan, that wasn't a request. It was a direction. Yes, you were delayed last week but you have a contract with the builder which you need to fulfil. If it's a matter of labour, I'll speak to Vic, but he'll deduct the cost of extra men from your fee."

"No need for that," spluttered Rowan.

"Excellent. Then I'll meet you on site at half past eight tomorrow morning."

"Can we make it half past nine?" Rowan pleaded.

"No, we can't. This is business. Set your alarm clock and get yourself out of bed."

She finished the call before he could protest further.

Nick laughed. "Where did Keya go?"

"What do you mean?" Keya bridled at the comment.

"Well it's not like you to be so assertive."

"If people say they're doing something, then they jolly well should, and not get all vague and uncertain about it."

"Someone's certainly woken up on the wrong, or maybe the right side of bed. Tea?" asked Nick.

"Please." Keya's shoulders slumped as she handed him her nearly empty cup. She might be more assertive, but she was still clumsy, and managing to land herself in awkward situations.

She switched her computer on and had just settled herself at her desk when Nick returned with Ryan.

"I thought you had most of the morning off," said Keya to Ryan, as Nick handed her a fresh cup of tea.

"I was up and about, so Mum suggested I help clean out the cupboard under the stairs if I had a spare hour." His cheeks flushed. "I pretended you'd sent me a message and scarpered. I hope you don't mind?" Ryan looked at Keya with large, pleading eyes.

"Actually, we have some news, so it's a good job you're here." Keya smiled warmly at him.

"What news?" asked Nick and Ryan in unison, as Keya stood up and walked across to the inspector's closed door. She knocked and opened it. "Sir, Ryan and Nick are here. Should we update them?"

"Good idea." Inspector Evans pushed back his chair. As Keya sat down, he walked across to the incident boards and removed the victims' names. Over the past few days, photographs, names of witnesses and suspects, and snippets of information had been pinned haphazardly to the boards.

"Close the door, Constable," directed the inspector.

Ryan shut the outer office door, and the general chatter and murmur of the police station was cut off.

In the silent team room, Inspector Evans pinned Katherine Dewsbury's name to the board, which had the photographs of the skeleton and waterwheel channel.

Nick and Ryan exchanged confused looks.

"This morning," began the inspector, "SOCO informed us that they have rerun DNA tests on the two bodies. They confirmed the skeleton is not Rachael Fawcett's, as we had all assumed, but a young Katherine Dewsbury. And they believe the woman who died in Keya's cafe's foundation trench is, in fact, Rachael Fawcett, who, up until Friday afternoon, was alive and well."

Inspector Evans pinned Rachael's name to the board showing a smiling picture of the woman Keya had known as Kate.

"I don't understand." Ryan spoke for all of them.

"Neither do I, Constable," agreed the inspector.

"I think it means," considered Nick, "that we are still looking at the same suspects and witnesses, but we need to do so from a different angle."

"Especially with Nathan Fawcett," suggested Ryan. "Surely he knew his sister was still alive."

"If it definitely was her and the DNA on file was correct," replied the inspector.

"Of course," cried Keya.

"What?" asked Ryan.

"The Welsh dragon."

"Don't you be blaming Y Ddraig Goch," protested Inspector Evans.

"What?" asked Keya.

"The red dragon," the inspector clarified.

"Oh, I wasn't, sir, but the coaster on your desk has a dragon on it. The same dragon symbol hanging from a silver chain I found on the chest of drawers in Kate's room at the pub."

"Wasn't Rachael's mother Welsh?" asked Ryan.

"She was," agreed Inspector Evans. "So you think the woman you know as Kate was given the necklace by her Welsh mother?"

"It's possible." Keya felt her pulse increase.

"I understand where you're coming from, but it's not conclusive evidence. She could have picked it up on a holiday in Wales."

But Keya was certain she was right.

"Back to Nathan Fawcett," announced the inspector, and Keya turned her thoughts away from young girls with dragon necklaces. "Keya, do you want to visit him again?"

"Yes." She looked from Nick to Ryan. "But would you mind if I take Nick? He can talk about cars and can be," Keya hesitated before adding, "more intimidating than either Ryan or I."

Nick stuck his chin out and straightened his back. "I can do intimidating." He pretended to crack his knuckles, but it just made him look ridiculous.

"And I'd like Ryan to use his computer skills to track down Kate's, no, Rachael's father. The man who moved to Scotland with the girl we now believe was Rachael."

"Mr Dewsbury?" asked Ryan.

"Yes, that's the one," Keya agreed.

"Surely he'd have known who his real daughter was?" insisted Nick.

They were all silent until Keya said, "We know he was really protective of his daughter and paranoid about losing her. What if he couldn't deal with Katherine's death and somehow persuaded Rachael to move to Scotland with him? We know she wanted a more exciting life than the one she had in Coln Akeman."

"Whatever the reason, we do need to locate Mr Dewsbury and find out why he kidnapped Rachael Fawcett," stated Inspector Evans.

"That sounds so serious. As if he took her against her will." Keya bit her lip and thought about a scared young girl being forced to leave her friends and her family and move to a strange place. It was serious.

Inspector Evans cleared his throat. "Our new line of questioning is on the basis that a young Rachael Fawcett left Coln Akeman thirty-one years ago. Potentially with Mr Dewsbury and, probably, after his daughter, Katherine, had died. We need to find out when she assumed Katherine's identity. Ryan, check the records for schools around where Mr Dewsbury settled once you have established where that was. And if you can't find Katherine, check for a Rachael Fawcett."

"We think Mr Dewsbury moved to Inverness, don't we, Ryan?" Keya looked across at her younger colleague.

"Yes. At the pub we found some old postcards from Mr Dewsbury to - what shall I call her?"

"Kate," suggested Keya, "since that's how she was known around here. If we start asking people about Rachael, they'll think we mean the girl from thirty years ago."

"OK. But no leaking this to the press," warned the inspector, narrowing his eyes at each of them in turn.

"The longer we keep this a secret, the easier it'll be for us. If," the inspector paused, "Kate's killer still believes we think she's Katherine, we're more likely to catch them off guard. And they may let something slip. I'll go back through all the interviews while Ryan looks for Mr Dewsbury, and you two interview Nathan Fawcett."

"And while we're at the car showroom, I'd like to speak to Wayne again," requested Keya. "If he killed Kate, it might have had nothing to do with the change in identities, but SOCO have moved the time of death forward and I want to check if he was working up until five thirty when he and his colleagues left for the pub."

"You know what you have to do," said the inspector as he removed Rachael's and Katherine's names from the incident boards. "Never know what prying eyes there are in a police station," he confided to Keya as she followed Nick out of their team room.

CHAPTER TWENTY-EIGHT

Keya climbed into Nick's metallic grey Mercedes, being careful not to scratch the door against the neighbouring car which was parked very close. On Nick's suggestion, she had changed out of her police uniform into civilian clothes.

"Let's keep this low-key and leave your squad car at the police station," said Nick. "Also, my car will convey a better impression to a man like Nathan Fawcett."

It was quiet at the showroom when they arrived and a team of men, Keya thought they were the mechanics, were cleaning and polishing the vehicles parked on the forecourt.

A red Porsche Cayenne roared into the dealership and parked beside the car showroom.

"Look out, the boss is here," called one of the men as he threw his sponge at a mate, who was leaning against a Range Rover smoking a cigarette.

Keya looked around the group before asking, "Is Wayne here today?"

"No, he called in sick. Is it right that lass he was seeing was murdered?" called the man from beside the Range Rover who was still smoking.

"I'm afraid so. Was Wayne here all Friday afternoon, before you went down to the Golden Miller?"

The man ground out his cigarette on the concrete forecourt. He didn't look at Keya.

"Answer the sergeant's question," instructed Nick stepping forward.

"Not sure," the man grumbled.

"Look," began Keya, "if he wasn't here there's no point pretending he was. We will find out and it will only make matters worse for him."

The man who had thrown the sponge admitted, "He disappeared halfway through the afternoon. Said he had to see someone."

"And when did he return?" Keya pressed.

"Just before we closed up," replied the man, squeezing water out of another large yellow sponge.

"And how did he seem?" Keya watched as the man wiped the sponge across the roof of a black car.

"Seem? I guess he was a bit quiet, now you mention it. Said he had to figure things out. If you don't mind?" The man looked over Keya's shoulder before hastily returning to wash the car.

"Looking for a new vehicle?" asked Nathan in his slimiest salesman's voice.

Keya and Nick turned to face him and, staring at Keya, Nathan took a step back.

Using their advantage, Keya and Nick strode towards him.

"This is my colleague, Sergeant Unwin," introduced Keya. "He knows a thing or two about cars. And about murder investigations."

Nathan crossed his arms. "If you're here with more questions about my sister, then I'd rather you just left things be. No good will come of raking up the past. Believe me."

"But the past doesn't stay buried, just like the girl's body we found. And then all sorts of secrets are revealed," Keya countered.

"Secrets? What sort of secrets?" Nathan's eyes darted from Keya to Nick.

"Like how long you've known your sister was alive," said Nick in a deadpan voice.

"I ... oh ... come inside."

Keya and Nick followed Nathan into the car showroom. The long-legged assistant was not around to greet them as they entered Nathan's office. He collapsed into the chair behind his glass-topped desk.

Nick and Keya remained standing, staring down at him.

"So, when did you realise your sister wasn't dead?" Nick asked again.

Nathan was pale as he replied, "I thought she was playing a trick at first, Rachael, when she disappeared as a kid. And that she'd walk back in with tales of adventures and the scrapes she'd got herself into, but as time went by Mum, Dad, and finally, I had to accept she wasn't coming home. Not long after that, we buried my dad and my mum moved back to Wales. I took over the pub, but it wasn't for me, and I sold it. Everything in my life had changed in less than two years. So I went away. Ran away, I guess you could say. To the other side of the world. I know it sounds like a cliché, but travelling and working my way around Australia was good for me, and so was the distance from the Cotswolds."

Nathan leaned forward and opened a desk drawer. He peered at something inside it but shook his head and closed it again.

Keya wondered if he had a bottle of something stashed inside the drawer.

Placing his arms on the desk, Nathan continued, "I returned to the UK after five years in Australia. There was still no news of Rachael, so it seemed the right thing to have her declared legally dead and move on. And that's what I did, until nine years after her death when I received a twenty first birthday card on Rachael's birthday, and then a card on my birthday. They fair freaked me out, but I was sure it was one of her schoolmates, Katherine or, more likely, Gilly, who'd sent them to me."

"Why did you think one of them would send you birthday cards?" asked Keya.

"To make sure I remembered, Rachael. So that neither they nor I would forget her." Nathan raised his eyebrows as if seeking an answer from Keya.

Nick leaned forward. "And you never tried to find out who was sending them to you?"

"How could I? The postmarks were always different. Sheffield,

Norwich, Manchester. And then suddenly they stopped arriving, about four years ago. And that worried me even more. What if Rachael had been sending me the cards and something had happened to her?"

"What did you do about it?" pressed Nick.

"Nothing," admitted Nathan.

"So you would have been delighted when Rachael returned to the Cotswolds."

"I couldn't …" Nathan stopped and pressed his lips together.

"No point stopping now," insisted Nick.

"I couldn't believe it at first."

"Did she come to see you?" asked Keya, her tone soft.

Nathan looked at her and there was a tear in his eye. He sniffed, "No. I was playing golf at the Spring Hills Hotel and my friend, the manager there, introduced her to me as Kate. She turned round and her face registered the same shock I felt, but she soon covered it up and greeted me politely, as if I was another guest. She was a good actress."

Or just good at covering up and hiding her feelings, thought Keya.

Nick stepped in front of a black leather chair and sat down as he asked, "How did you recognise her after all these years?"

"She was introduced as Kate Dewsbury, but Katherine never had those bright intelligent eyes. She was mouse-like and blonde against Rachael's dark hair and outgoing nature."

Keya also pulled a chair across and sat down in front of Nathan's glass desk. "But it could have been any Katherine Dewsbury, not the one you'd known as a child."

Nathan shrugged. "Maybe it was hearing the name which made me think of Rachael, or perhaps it was the silver necklace of a Welsh dragon she was wearing round her neck. Like the one Mum gave Rachael. Or maybe it was just the same shock of recognition in her eyes. But it was Rachael. I spoke to her after my disastrous round of golf."

Nathan paused, so Keya pressed gently, "What did she say?"

"Not a lot. She was serving customers, but she did ask if I'd received her cards, and apologised for not sending them recently. I asked why she was calling herself Kate Dewsbury and she told me it was a long story. Then she was called to another table, and I was joined by Neil Cleavely."

"Did you try to make contact with her again?" asked Nick.

"I returned to play golf the following week, but she wasn't there, and nobody would give me her number. I was busy negotiating for the second showroom in Cheltenham, so it was another month before I went back to the hotel. This time to meet Neil."

"And did you see Rachael then?" Nick pressed his lips together and, although his voice was calm, Keya knew he was becoming frustrated with Nathan.

"I did, and I slipped up and called her Rachael. Neil wanted to know why, so I told him she looked like my sister, or something like that. And the next time I went back for a Christmas party, she wasn't there, and the receptionist told me she'd left."

"Did you try to find her?" asked Keya.

"I didn't see the point. She knew where I was and would find me if she wanted to. After all these years, I wasn't chasing after her. Besides, I was busy with work."

Nick narrowed his eyes. "Did she ask you for anything, like money?"

Nathan shifted his ample frame in his chair but replied, "No, she didn't. But that didn't surprise me. She was always the resourceful type. As a child, she often persuaded punters at the pub to buy her a packet of crisps or a bar of chocolate."

Anger and frustration swelled up in Keya at Nathan's nonchalant manner. She leaned forward, grabbed the table and, raising her voice, demanded, "So you just let your sister, who you thought had died thirty years ago, walk back out of your life?"

Nathan shrank back and, in a small voice, replied, "I told you. Work. It was my priority."

Keya and Ryan didn't get anything else of use out of Nathan. He refused to answer any more of their questions.

As they walked out of the showroom Keya sounded resentful as she demanded, "Can you believe he would act so callously?"

"I can, but I don't believe everything Nathan told us. He was hiding something. I'm just not sure what. And I know it's your case, but how about we both visit Spring Hills Hotel?"

"Good idea," agreed Keya, trudging back to Nick's car.

CHAPTER TWENTY-NINE

The wind buffeted Nick's Mercedes as he drove expertly and quickly to Stow-on-the-Wold, cut across to Chipping Norton, and took the road to Banbury, turning off before the Oxfordshire town to Lower Tadmarton and the Spring Hills Hotel.

As on Keya's previous visit, the three flags beside the entrance cracked against their flag poles and the same receptionist, this time with too much purple eyeshadow, greeted Nick with a flutter of her long, mascaraed eyelashes.

She barely glanced at Keya until Nick announced they were police officers.

Looking down at Keya, in a literal and metaphorical manner, the receptionist said in a waspish tone, "You were here before, with that young policeman. At least you're not wearing uniforms this time."

Dismissing Keya, she returned her attention to Nick and said, "Mrs Cleavely's in her office."

"No, I'm not, I'm here," announced Mrs Cleavely, walking towards the reception desk. "How can I help you, officers?" She wore a simple pale green shift dress and a matching jacket.

Nick stepped forward and said, "When my colleagues visited before, your husband told them you had dismissed Katherine Dewsbury, but didn't give a reason why."

"He told you that, did he?" Mrs Cleavely shook her head, her lips pressed together in either annoyance or disappointment; Keya wasn't sure which.

"I was very happy with Katherine's work, and I was disappointed when she left during our busy Christmas period. Neil told me she had chosen to leave, but I didn't believe him. But staff come and go all the time and I'm too busy to spend time wondering about any one of them in particular. I found a replacement for her, and the hotel continues to operate under my steady hand."

She raised her head, standing taller.

Keya thought her unspoken words were that the hotel operated despite her husband.

"Thank you," Keya said to Mrs Cleavely. "Then it's your husband we need to see. Is he in the fitness centre?"

Mrs Cleavely looked across at the receptionist who pursed her lips, but her eyes gave her away, so without waiting for a reply, Keya turned and entered the corridor which led to the rear of the hotel, via the entrance to the dining room.

"He's busy at the moment," called the receptionist.

Nick was jogging as he caught up with Keya.

"I'm sure he is," Keya muttered.

Neil wasn't in the main gym, but they heard loud music and shouting from somewhere to their right.

They weaved their way around fitness machines. A young man with a tight-fitting white t-shirt held Nick's gaze and lifted his chin when they passed, while the eyes of the young woman at the neighbouring machine lingered on Nick.

Keya might as well have been invisible.

A plain white door, disguised as a wall panel, was ajar and they heard the music through it. Keya would have peered into the room, but Nick nonchalantly pulled the door open to reveal the startled faces of eight women, varying in age from around sixty to over eighty.

One woman, with blue-tinted hair, cried, "Are you coming to join us?"

Nick smiled, "Sorry ladies. He held up his warrant card. We've come to speak to Mr Cleavely."

Keya presumed Nick knew by the description she'd given him that the man who'd been waving his arms about at the front of the fitness room was Neil Cleavely, although with his fluffy blue headband she wasn't sure she'd have placed him immediately.

"Naughty, naughty," crooned one of the other women and several of her friends giggled.

Neil gave Nick and Keya a frightened glance before returning his attention to his class.

"Well done, ladies. Let's call it a day. I'll leave you to complete your stretches while I talk to the officers." Neil approached a black electronic box and pressed a switch and then turned a dial as softer, relaxing music filled the studio.

The women continued to whisper as Keya and Nick left the studio, accompanied by Neil, who'd wrapped a small blue towel, which matched his sweatband, around his neck.

"My office," he growled as he led them from the room. His office was just as untidy as last time Keya had been in it, although there were no unopened cardboard boxes.

Keya found a red padded stool, which looked as if it belonged to a piece of gym equipment, and sat down. Nick found a wooden chair and Neil pulled a similar one out from under a small wooden desk, pushed against the side wall.

"What is so important that you have to interrupt one of my classes?" demanded Neil, a vein throbbing in his neck.

"I don't think you were entirely truthful when my colleagues interviewed you about Katherine Dewsbury's death."

The sweat continued to glisten on Neil's face, but he lost his flush. "But I had nothing to do with it. I was here, at the hotel, all last Friday. That was when she was killed wasn't it?"

Did he protest too much, wondered Keya.

Nick ignored his question. "You said your wife dismissed Katherine, but that's not true, is it? You sacked her. And refused to give her a reference. Why?"

Neil removed his sweatband and wiped his forehead with it. He turned to his desk, picked up a plastic water bottle and drank from it.

As Keya watched, she actually felt sorry for him. He was older than he first appeared with lines on his face and perhaps he kept his hair short to hide the scattering of grey hairs above his ears.

The older ladies in his class might fawn over him, but the younger women would be more likely to find him creepy. The image of him with this morning's class made her laugh. Quickly, she clamped her hand over her mouth.

"Sergeant," rebuked Nick in surprise.

"You weren't having an affair with Kate," stated Keya. "You might have wanted to, but it wasn't the reason you dismissed her."

Neil looked deflated and Keya realised that, despite the outfit and pretence of strutting around the gym, he was a coward. She pressed home her advantage. "Did Kate find out something she shouldn't, and you had to get rid of her?"

Keya glanced at the white plastic containers stacked on the floor beside the rear shelves.

"No, nothing like that," spluttered Neil, glancing nervously at the containers.

"So what was it?" Nick asked in a conversational tone.

"It was one of the guests. She upset him," Neil blurted.

"And how did she do that?" Nick asked, keeping his voice level.

Neil clamped his lips together.

"Mr Cleavely, if you want to do this the hard way, we'll take you with us back to Cirencester police station, and when we've finished, you can find your own way home." Nick sounded bored.

"It was one of my business clients. Someone I hope to work with more in the future. Someone I don't want to upset. He and Kate recognised each other after we'd played a round of golf. Then, whenever he returned, Kate made an excuse to be somewhere else, but I interrupted them one day. There was something between them, but I didn't like to pry."

"You thought they were having an affair?" suggested Nick.

"More that they had had, and it was now over. They were rather awkward around each other. So when my client gave me an envelope and asked me to get rid of Kate, without a reference, I didn't like to refuse."

"How much was in the envelope?" demanded Keya, annoyed that Neil had sacked Kate for money and taken away her means of supporting herself.

Nick gave her a warning look, and she bit her lip.

"£2,000. I guess he had a strong reason for wanting rid of her."

"So you gave her the sack. Just before Christmas." Keya tried but failed to keep her tone level.

Neil shrugged. "It was business."

"And do you still see this client?" Nick was finding it easier to maintain his professional manner.

"Sometimes," replied Neil, evasively.

There was something else, thought Keya. Fear. What was Neil afraid of?

"And when was the last time?" pressed Nick.

Neil turned back to his desk and drank from his water bottle.

"How long will it take to get back to the police station?" Nick asked casually.

"All right!" exclaimed Neil. "It was Friday. Friday afternoon. We played golf together."

Keya frowned. If Nathan was the man who Neil was covering for, and they had been playing golf, it was unlikely Nathan would have had time to drive to Akemans and kill Kate.

"To confirm," said Nick, "you were playing golf with Nathan Fawcett on Friday afternoon."

Neil's eyes widened. "I never said it was Nathan," he squawked.

"But it was." Nick spoke slowly and levelly.

At last Neil seemed to dredge up some courage, and he stuck his chin out as he replied, "So what if I was playing golf with an important client on Friday?"

Neil refused to say any more and Nick and Keya left his office. Keya felt a lump of disappointment in her stomach.

"Why don't I believe him?" muttered Nick.

Keya felt the lump flutter. "You don't?"

"Something doesn't ring true. Do you mind if we check the golf records while we're here?"

"Why? What do you expect to find?'

"I'm not sure. It's just a hunch."

The golf clubhouse was signposted when they left the fitness centre, and they followed a gravel path along the side of the lake.

The single-storey brick clubhouse was raised up and had a deck running along the front of it where golfers could sit and watch other players.

"That'll be the eighteenth hole," said Nick as they followed the path past a red flag and climbed four wooden steps into the building.

"Hello," greeted a fresh-faced man in his early twenties.

Nick flashed his warrant card and said, "Was Mr Cleavely playing on Friday afternoon with a guest?"

The young man turned back the pages of the ledger on the desk and ran his finger down it. "Three o'clock tee off," he read.

Keya felt the knot reform in her stomach.

"And the guest was Mr Fawcett?" enquired Nick.

"The carman," agreed the young man. And then he frowned. "He usually arrives in a smart red Porsche SUV but this time the caddy complained he had to drag the clubs individually out of the back of a small Fiat Punto." The young man ran his hand along the ledger. "Strange, there's no record of his round. He must have lost his scorecard, or forgotten to hand it in."

"Perhaps," agreed Nick. "Thank you for your help."

The young man smiled back at him. "And if you ever fancy a round of golf …"

"Not my sport, but thank you."

As they descended the wooden clubhouse steps, Keya asked, "What did that mean?"

"That while Nathan Fawcett started his round of golf, he didn't necessarily finish it. And don't you find it interesting that he wasn't driving his own conspicuous car?"

CHAPTER THIRTY

"I'm hungry," complained Keya as she climbed into Nick's car.

"It is half past two, so I'm not surprised," replied Nick, settling himself in the driver's seat. "I noticed a garage about five miles back on the road to Chipping Norton. But if you do eat in my car, don't drop crumbs."

Keya sank back in the leather seat, suitably chastised.

They did stop at the garage, and she carefully ate a limp egg mayonnaise sandwich on nondescript white bread as Nick drove them back to Cirencester. Arriving at the station just after half past three, Keya felt droplets of drizzle from the grey sky.

"How did you get on?" asked Ryan when Keya entered the team room.

He was sitting at a desk with a pad of lined paper beside him, the front sheet covered in scribbled notes.

There was a white oblong plastic table, the folding sort, in the gap left by the removal of the extra desk next to Ryan. It was covered in papers, some scattered about, and others arranged in piles.

Ryan must have noticed Keya staring at the table as he said, "The inspector's gone back through the file, as well as our notes and reports. He said he's sorting them the old-fashioned way. Anyway, I'm glad you're back. You'll be able to join the Skype call."

"What Skype call?" asked Keya.

Ryan tapped his pad with a pen. "I've been phoning around the Scottish Highlands, and I eventually found the junior school Kate attended when she first moved to Scotland. It's a tiny village one, east of Inverness and only has one full-time teacher. The current teacher, Gail, is young and doesn't remember Kate but, as luck would have it, or perhaps this sort of thing happens in the north of Scotland, her mum was the previous teacher. So Gail is going to her mum's after school finishes and organising a Skype call in, " Ryan checked his watch, "about ten minutes."

Nick entered the room as Inspector Evans opened his door and, standing with his arms folded, asked, "So what did you find out?"

"That Nathan knew his sister's new identity, and that she was living and working in the area," replied Nick as he removed his suit jacket and hung it on a peg he'd drilled into the wall behind his desk.

"And his alibi might have holes in it," added Keya.

Ryan's computer started ringing. "That'll be Gail, and hopefully her mum."

"Who?" asked Nick.

"A schoolteacher from Scotland," explained Keya.

"Who wants to join me?" Ryan shifted his chair to one side.

"Me," said Keya enthusiastically as she grabbed the blue fabric chair from behind her desk and rolled it across to Ryan's. "Excuse me," she said to Inspector Evans, who stepped back into his office.

"Sergeant Unwin, you can finish telling me about your enquiries while Sergeant Varma and Constable Jenkins talk to the computer."

Nick raised his eyebrows at Keya as she positioned her chair and he followed the inspector into his office, closing the door behind him.

"Hi, Gail," said Ryan as Keya sat down. "This is my colleague, Sergeant Varma."

Gail had a pleasant face and soft Scottish accent, very similar to Kate's.

The image on the screen panned out to include an elderly lady with a stern expression.

"And this is my mum," introduced Gail.

"You can call me Mrs MacDonald," instructed the older lady in a stronger Scottish accent.

Keya smiled. How wonderful! A proper Scot. She wondered if Mrs MacDonald's hair had been a coppery-red when she was younger.

"Gail says you want to speak about Katherine Dewsbury," announced Mrs MacDonald, getting straight to the point and interrupting Keya's reverie.

"Yes, Mrs MacDonald. Did you teach her?" asked Keya politely.

"Aye, but only for a year. Then she moved up to High School in Nairn. She was a bonnie lassie, and she didn't lack intelligence, but she dinnae like schoolwork. Boys. That was all she was interested in, which made her da furious. A strange relationship they had, mind you. I'm not sure what happened to her ma, nobody ever said.

"But Katherine and her da were more like equals and in the end, he gave up. Katherine left school as soon as she could and worked in a department store in Inverness. I can't tell you much more, except I heard she and her da had a huge row when she was in her early twenties, and she moved back to England. I dinnae hear any more from her."

Keya leaned towards the screen and said, "That's very helpful, Mrs MacDonald. I'd just like to check we're talking about the same girl." She looked at Ryan, who pointed to a photograph of a young Rachael Fawcett, which was lying on the plastic table beside her. She picked it up and held it in front of the computer screen.

"Up a bit for the camera," instructed Ryan.

"Och aye, that's Katherine," confirmed Mrs MacDonald.

Lowering the photo, Keya asked, "Do we have a photo of Mr Dewsbury?"

Ryan shook his head.

Mrs MacDonald said, "It was such a shame when the mill closed down three years ago. Many men, like Katherine's father, lost their jobs. I heard he moved south."

"Mr Dewsbury?" checked Keya.

"Aye. I guess with no Katherine and no job, there was nothing keeping him here. He was English, after all."

"Do you have any idea where he went?"

"Sorry." The older lady shook her head.

"You've been very helpful. Thank you," said Keya.

"Nae problem," responded Mrs MacDonald, before looking across at her daughter.

"Did that help?" asked Gail, focusing the camera on herself. "Sorry, there isn't much we can tell you."

"You confirmed Katherine was in Scotland, which is important to our case," replied Ryan.

"Has something happened to Katherine?" They heard the older lady ask.

Gail smiled sadly at them and finished the call.

Keya sat back and said, "So we know Rachael moved to Scotland with a man calling himself Mr Dewsbury, who we presume was Katherine's father, and Rachael assumed Katherine's identity."

"And she stayed there for about ten years before leaving the area, if what Mrs MacDonald said is true," added Ryan, "and from what I gathered today, the communities up there are small, and people know other people's business."

"So that just leaves the last twenty years unaccounted for," pondered Keya.

"I can try to track her jobs," suggested Ryan, "but if she was paid cash, there might be no trace of them."

"I'm not sure we need to do that yet," considered Keya. "We know she moved to Scotland and lived there. And we know she was back in this area by March last year, working at the Spring Hills Hotel, and then at my local pub. We should concentrate on who she's met since March. And we should also try to find her father … I mean, Mr Dewsbury. If he knew Kate was back in the area, he might have moved back too."

CHAPTER THIRTY-ONE

Inspector Evans' office door opened, and Nick walked out into the team room.

Once again, the inspector stood in his doorway and asked, "What did you find out from your contact in Scotland, Constable?"

Ryan glanced at Keya before replying, "That Rachael Fawcett, as Katherine Dewsbury, attended a local school and lived just outside Inverness until her early twenties. Apparently, she moved away after a row with her 'father', although we don't know where to."

"What next?" asked the inspector.

Keya stood up and moved round to the back of her chair. "I've asked Ryan to look into Kate's friends and acquaintances since March last year, when she started working at the Spring Hills Hotel. And we also need to find Mr Dewsbury, as we believe he left Scotland two or three years ago and may have moved back to the area."

"I'll take the lead on that," offered Nick. "Finding him is a priority in his daughter's case. I thought I might speak to Tim Simmonds again, since he seems to remember people and events from around the time the two girls disappeared."

Keya glanced at her watch. It was nearly half past four. "And I want to see if I can find Wayne Hourigan."

"Do you need me?" asked Ryan, hopefully.

"No, I think I'll be OK, but thanks for the offer," replied Keya.

"Very well," declared Inspector Evans. "You two go and conduct your interviews," he looked from Keya to Nick and then to Ryan, "and, Constable, don't work too late this afternoon. I've a few old contacts I want to see if I can catch up with, so I'll see you all in the morning." He turned back into his office.

That would be Tuesday morning, Keya realised.

"Actually," she raised, "I've a site meeting first thing, to finally remove the waterwheel. And I want to speak to Vic Peters and his men about the case."

Inspector Evans reappeared and said, "Then let's aim for half past eleven to review progress with the cases."

Keya left the police station and drove back to Nathan Fawcett's showroom. There was no sign of Nathan's red Porsche Cayenne, but as she parked her own VW Polo, Wayne Hourigan drove onto the forecourt in a black Fiat Punto, with 'Fawcett's Courtesy Car' printed on the side.

Wayne climbed out and walked across to Keya. "I heard you were asking after me." He looked across at the main showroom building before adding, "and that you upset the boss."

"Did we?" queried Keya.

"The lads said he left soon after you and your colleague, and we haven't seen him since. And his car's not here."

Keya looked across at the car Wayne had been driving. "Does he ever drive that one?" she asked.

Wayne looked at the concrete forecourt and shuffled his feet.

"Only a witness told us he was driving a car like that last Friday."

"I wouldn't know," mumbled Wayne.

Keya narrowed her eyes and tilted her head to one side. "Why wouldn't you? Where were you on Friday afternoon?"

"Look, you only asked me where I was from five thirty, so I haven't lied to you."

"But?" pressed Keya.

"OK, I went to meet Kate." He held his arms up in a gesture of surrender. "To try to persuade her not to move out."

"Did you have an argument?"

"No, nothing like that. But she said she wasn't sure she was going to stay in the area, and that she needed time to think."

"Had she mentioned leaving and moving on to you before?"

"No, in fact, she'd told me she was happy to be back home, and she wanted to stay here. So I asked her what had changed and, at first, she refused to tell me. I thought there must be another man, and in a way, I was right." Wayne tugged at his checked shirt.

"What way?" Keya's voice rose in pitch.

"She said she'd met her brother and her dad."

"And?"

"And that was it. She wouldn't tell me any more. She threw the last of her things into a bin bag and rushed down the stairs with it. She did tell me she'd be in touch, but she had to work out what to do. I followed her, and outside she stopped and let me catch up. Then she kissed me on the cheek and said she'd been running all her life, but now it was time to stop. It was time to put things right, so she could move on. I had no idea what she was on about, but I really thought she'd come back. Maybe she would have. But now I'll never know."

Keya felt a lump in her throat and as she placed her hand on Wayne's checked sleeve, she said, "I'm really sorry. Do you know what time Kate left you?"

"Just after four. I rushed back to work but I needn't have worried about being missed. The boss wasn't around."

Keya thanked Wayne and called Ryan before she drove home.

"Is everything OK?" he asked, his voice full of concern.

"Yes, I'm fine. I actually feel sorry for Wayne, for losing Kate. But he did tell me some interesting things." Keya relayed her conversation with Wayne. "And it appears that Mr Dewsbury is in the area."

"I'll speak to Nick in the morning and see what Tim Simmonds told him, and I'll start searching for Mr Dewsbury."

"Great, have a good night, and I'll see you in the morning."

As Keya drove steadily home, she wondered just what surprises the next day would bring.

CHAPTER THIRTY-TWO

Keya arrived at the cafe building site at Akemans keen and early at eight o'clock on Tuesday morning. As she was also conducting police business, she'd decided to wear her police uniform.

She found the relevant section of metal fencing open and walked towards the back of the old mill building.

Inside, she found Vic Peters standing outside his office door with his workmen standing or sitting around on wooden benches, facing him.

"Welcome, Keya," he greeted her as she joined them. "Help yourself to tea. Are Rowan and his gang definitely coming this morning?"

"I made it clear we expected them in," she glanced at her watch, "less than thirty minutes."

Keya approached the metal urn of hot water. Brad removed his vintage style motorbike helmet from the table so she could reach the mugs.

Vic instructed, "Brad and Dave, you be on hand to help Rowan. We need to make sure his team actually removes the waterwheel this time. Then we can start knocking that wall down." He pointed to the end wall with his free hand. The other clasped a mug, which he raised to his mouth.

Keya poured hot water into her own mug.

With her back to Vic, she heard him say, "Shane and Shawn. You two finish the extension foundations. Has anyone seen the plasterers?"

Mutterings of "No" came from the builders.

"Then I'd better chase them. We're behind in here and I need this plastering finished by the end of the week. Any questions?"

Keya removed her tea bag, dropped it into a plastic bucket with a white bin liner, and turned to face Vic.

"Yeah, do the police know how that woman who was found in the trench died?" one of the builders called out.

Vic looked at Keya, who glanced around the group. Several builders turned towards her.

Keya took a deep breath and said, "Unfortunately, the victim, Katherine Dewsbury, was murdered."

Ignoring the gasps and expletives, Keya asked, "Did any of you see her, or anyone else, hanging around the building site on Friday afternoon as you were leaving?"

"In the morning, there was that man we saw during our site meeting," suggested Vic.

"Yes," agreed Keya. All the builders were now looking at her. She asked, "Did any of you see or speak to him? He was stocky, and wearing a tweed jacket and cap."

"That doesn't exactly narrow it down. Not round here," called one of the builders.

"Well, if you do think of anything, I shall be around for a while, making sure we don't find any more bodies when we remove the waterwheel." She tried but failed to make her comment sound humorous. Two bodies on one building site was no laughing matter.

The builders stood up and collected their hard hats and boxes of tools. The phone rang in Vic's office, and he left to answer it.

Keya gulped down half her tea before putting it to one side and grabbing a hard hat and high-vis jacket. She wandered outside and made her way down the temporary steps to the edge of the river.

A small piece of crime scene tape, attached to the rusty drainpipe, still fluttered in the wind. The larger piece was wrapped around the post beside the river. The waterwheel stood forlorn and lonely.

She had a desire to lean over the stone bridge of the water channel to touch it, but pulled her hand back, feeling slightly ridiculous. She prayed it would be removed without revealing any more secrets or dead bodies.

"I saw that fellow you were asking about last Friday," said Brad, interrupting her thoughts.

"Of course, Vic sent you to deal with him, and the victim, or at least I presume the woman who we saw walking down the river was the victim."

Brad squinted. "I wouldn't know about that. There was a woman, but she left when she saw me."

"Did you recognise the man?"

"Not then, but I did when he came back in the afternoon."

Keya took a deep breath and gave Brad her full attention. "When was that?" she asked.

"As I was shutting up the site. Vic and the others had left, and it's my job to make sure none of them leave any tools lying around, that the power is switched off, and that the site is secure. He drove a little black car round the back of the auction building and parked close to the site entrance. It had 'Fawcett's Courtesy Car' printed on the car door and that's when I recognised him, from leaflets I've seen. It was the car dealer, Nathan Fawcett."

"And was he alone?"

"I think so. I couldn't see anyone in the car with him. He got out, looked around, but when he saw me, he got back in and reversed the car back the way he'd come. But as I rode out, having secured the site, I saw his car in the car park, but there was no sign of him."

"And the woman?" asked Keya.

"Which one? There were quite a few of them coming out of the antiques centre."

"The woman who walked past the building site to the river in the morning?"

Brad kicked at a stone and muttered, "No, she wasn't one of them."

Keya heard a gaggle of voices and she turned to watch the exceptionally tall and willowy figure of Rowan, dressed in fluorescent orange trousers, approach them, leading his team.

"No need to arrest us. We're on time," joked Rowan, who towered over both Keya and Brad.

"Good," said Keya before adding, "Thank you. Brad and one of the other builders will help with any equipment or extra manpower you need this morning. Those are Vic's instructions."

"I've buoyed the gang up, so let's get straight on with it." Rowan turned to his helpers, who were carrying various pieces of equipment, including what looked like a small chain saw.

"Are you just going to chop it up?" Keya blurted in surprise.

"This isn't the original wheel," explained Rowan. "That would have rotted away. The paddles on this one are secured with large metal bolts which have mostly rusted in situ, so we'll have to cut them away."

Keya pressed her lips together in disappointment. She'd had romantic visions of the old waterwheel being lovingly restored back to life.

"Don't worry," reassured Rowan. 'It won't have cheap imitation paddles. They'll all be oak, just like the original." He turned to Brad. "I'll need scaffolding poles and planks so we can create an access platform around the wheel."

Brad walked back up the temporary steps as Rowan added, "There's no point you hanging around. I promise we'll work diligently, but this morning's progress will be slow as we build the supporting structure around the wheel. Hopefully, we can start removing paddles this afternoon."

"How long will it take?" asked Keya.

"We've scheduled three days, but hopefully we'll be done in two and a half. And I'll take some of the paddles back with me this evening so my craftsman can start work on making new ones while we finish on site."

"It's all clear down here," called up the woman with the shaved head who Keya remembered was an archaeologist.

"Excellent, and here come the first scaffolding poles."

Brad was stooping under the weight of the scaffolding poles and Keya realised he was probably in his sixties. Why wasn't he enjoying his retirement rather than lugging round heavy metal poles on a building site?

CHAPTER THIRTY-THREE

Feeling disappointed that she was missing the action and the removal of the waterwheel, Keya drove to Cirencester police station.

As she entered the team room Ryan looked up and grinned at her. "I've made loads of progress this morning and you'll never guess what?"

"What?" Keya stopped in front of Ryan's desk.

"Our prosperous car salesman is not doing as well as he likes to make out. Both his house and his business are mortgaged to the max."

"So his business is failing?"

"No, I wouldn't say that. In the latest set of accounts I can access, which are eighteen months old, the business was doing well, but it's changed its address since they were filed."

Nick entered the room carrying a mug of coffee. He said, "That's probably the move to Burford Road, and there's the new showroom in Cheltenham."

Keya remembered the conversation with her future brother-in-law the previous Saturday. "He's also looking for a site in Gloucester."

"Unless his profits have drastically improved, that's really going to stretch the business."

"Let me see if I can find out any more about it." Keya pulled her phone out of her pocket and called her sister.

"Well done, Keya. You've remembered we have another fitting this afternoon," Zivah said when she answered the call.

Keya had completely forgotten. "Same time and place?" she asked vaguely.

"Don't you remember? We moved it back to five as you said you were unlikely to make four thirty."

"Oh, yes, of course." Keya was distracted as Ryan pointed excitedly at his screen. Nick walked across to join him.

"Zivah, could you send me Aadi's phone number?"

"Why?" Zivah sounded defensive. "What are you two planning?"

"It's nothing to do with the wedding. This is business. I need to follow up a lead. Something he told me about on Saturday night."

"You're not getting him into trouble, are you?" Zivah's voice rose.

"No, Zivah. I just need to ask him about someone his company might be doing business with."

Ryan scribbled on the pad beside him and looked excitedly up at Nick. What had they found?

"Look Zivah, if you don't want to send it to me, I'll call the company he works for."

"There's no need to be like that."

Keya sighed.

Zivah continued in a disapproving tone. "I don't understand what you do. Why do you want to be getting mixed up with dead bodies and other people's work? Why can't you do something nice?"

"I am trying to. I'm setting up the cafe. But my police work is important too. It's not all bad. I help people as well."

Nick knocked on Inspector Evans' door.

"Look, I have to go. If you want to, send me the number. If not, I'll find Aadi another way." She finished the call before her sister could protest and followed Ryan as he entered Inspector Evan's office.

Nick was already standing inside, facing the inspector, who looked up at them from behind his desk.

"So tell me about this breakthrough you two have had," instructed the inspector, leaning back in his chair.

"It's Katherine Dewsbury's father," explained Nick and he glanced across at Ryan.

Ryan continued, "The old lady, Kate's former schoolteacher, told us the mill he'd been working at had closed down and she thought he'd moved back to England."

"And Keya said that as Kate was living in the Cotswolds, he might be drawn back here," said Nick.

"But when I searched for men called Dewsbury, there was nobody with that name in Gloucestershire. It's not a common surname. There are a cluster of them in the West Midlands, who our Dewsbury family may be related to ..."

"So?" interrupted the inspector.

Ryan's cheeks flushed. "Nick suggested I look at similar names. In the Inverness-shire registry, there was a Bradley Daresbury living in the Nairn District. And I've found a Bradley Daresbury living in Cirencester. He's in his sixties and moved to the area three years ago, which fits."

Bradley wasn't a particularly common name either, thought Keya. And it could be shortened to Brad.

She realised Inspector Evans was staring at her. "Something you want to add, Sergeant?"

"Do we know if Bradley Daresbury has a job, and if so, where?" she asked.

"No, I don't have that info yet," replied Ryan. "Is it important?"

"It might be. There's an older man called Brad who's working as part of the building crew at the cafe site. Could be a coincidence?"

"Or not," grunted the inspector. "See what you can find out, Constable."

Keya turned to leave.

"Just a minute, Sergeant," called Inspector Evans.

Keya stepped to one side so Ryan could pass.

"You were having an animated phone call. Was it about the case?" asked the inspector.

"Not exactly," replied Keya. "I'm trying to track down my future brother-in-law, as he might know something about Nathan Fawcett's business and financial situation."

Inspector Evans raised his eyebrows.

"He told me Nathan was interested in a site his company owns for another car showroom."

"Nathan Fawcett certainly sees himself as a mover and shaker in the high-end car dealership business," responded the inspector, dryly. "But what does this have to do with the case?"

"I'm not sure," admitted Keya. "But I found out today …" She hesitated, realising it was Brad who'd given her the information, "that a witness might have seen Nathan at the building site on Friday afternoon. And as we don't think his golfing alibi is that strong, he could have been at Akemans instead, meeting our victim."

Keya thought about Kate and her brother. Kate was a waitress at a pub earning hardly enough to live on, while Nathan had a large house on an exclusive estate, with an expanding business empire. And yet, when Nick had asked Nathan if Kate had asked him for money, he said she hadn't.

And Keya thought that was true. She thought it more likely that Kate would want to maintain her independence and make her own way, but still, with Nathan and his flash car. Keya was confused and couldn't work out what she thought was the truth.

"What is it, Sergeant?"

Keya glanced from the inspector to Nick. Both of them were looking at her expectantly.

"I don't know. With Nathan involved, I keep thinking it must be about money, but I just can't see Kate asking him for any. Not now, after all these years."

They were all silent.

"Not now, after all these years," repeated Keya, almost to herself.

From the room next door, they heard Ryan say, "Thank you, Vic, and I'll pass on to Keya that progress is being made with the waterwheel." There was a pause before Ryan joked, "And yes, no more bodies. That is good news." Ryan finished his call.

"You were right, Keya, Sergeant Varma," Ryan corrected himself as he entered the inspector's office, his eyes flashing with excitement.

"The foreman at the cafe site confirmed that Brad's full name is Bradley Daresbury and that he started working for the company three years ago when he moved down from Scotland. He doesn't do any skilled labour, but he sets things out, clears up, and generally gets on with anything he's tasked to do. Vic, the foreman, says he's a real asset to the team. But he did admit he's quiet and keeps to himself."

"So where does this put us now?" asked Inspector Evans.

Nick answered. "If Bradley Dewsbury or Daresbury has been in the area for as long as, if not longer than, Kate, then he could have known where she was and tried to make contact with her."

"It's possible," replied the inspector.

"Except …" Keya considered the site meeting the previous week. "If it was Kate who I saw last week at Akemans, then Brad definitely saw her. And I remember now, he and the woman did appear to recognise each other, although they didn't speak, and she left quickly."

"So if Kate was in contact with her real brother and her assumed father, then either one of them could have killed her," surmised Nick.

"Not after all these years," repeated Keya vaguely, for the second time.

"What do you mean by that?" asked Ryan.

Inspector Evans answered. "I think what Keya is trying to say is that we need to look at this in the context of the original case and the disappearance of Rachael Fawcett, and what we now know was the death of Katherine Dewsbury."

Ryan protested, "But according to the reports, neither Nathan nor Mr Dewsbury were in Coln Akeman at the time."

Inspector Evans glanced across at the still nameless incident boards. "I think," he considered, "we should follow up the newer leads for the moment."

Keya's phone rang. She checked the screen, but the number was unknown. "Can I take this?" She looked up at the inspector, who nodded.

"Sergeant Varma," she answered the call formally as she walked out of the inspector's office.

"Keya, it's Aadi. Zivah said you wanted to speak to me."

"I do. Thanks for calling." Keya was surprised by the call. She hadn't expected Aadi to take the time to contact her.

"And she said it was official business, and nothing to do with the wedding." Aadi laughed. "Which seemed to confuse her, but bless my dear fiancée, all she can think about at the moment is our wedding."

Keya felt her feelings towards her sister soften, but she was also frustrated that Zivah was living in a bubble with herself at the centre. But maybe it was best to shield her and Maitri from crimes like those she was currently investigating.

"So what did you want to speak to me about?" asked Aadi.

"Nathan Fawcett. You said he was interested in some land for another car showroom."

There was a pause before Aadi asked tentatively, "Is he involved in any criminal activities?"

Keya thought of Mr Finch's quad bike. "Do you mean handling stolen goods? Not that we are aware of, but he is a person of interest in one of our cases." And before Aadi had time to respond, she continued hastily, "And we're interested in his financial situation. One of my colleagues thinks he's stretched to the limit and has mortgaged everything he owns."

"That's a very astute analysis," confirmed Aadi in a serious tone. "My bosses have refused to build bespoke premises for him to lease, although they have offered to sell him a site at the edge of our development. His business is profitable, and he might ride out his current cash flow restrictions, as long as nothing impacts his business."

Like the death of his sister, thought Keya. But that was likely to affect him personally more than professionally. But if Kate had demanded money, that would be a different story.

"Keya, is that all? I've got to run to a meeting."

"That's great, Aadi. Thanks again for calling."

"And don't forget Zivah's dress fitting this afternoon. She might act as if she doesn't care if you're there for her or not, but in reality, she relies on her older sister. She wants you to share her happy event."

"I'll be there."

Keya finished the call, smiling. Aadi was right. She did want to share her sister's happiness.

Sharing. Siblings. Money.

"Ryan," she called. "When Nathan's dad died, he passed the pub to Nathan, who then sold it, and for a large amount."

"That's right." Ryan leaned over the plastic table next to him and picked up a piece of paper. "For £300,000."

"And he took all that money?"

"I'm not sure if he gave some to his mum."

"Can you check the will?"

"Sure, but I don't think it's here. I'll have to check probate records for that year."

Nick walked out of Inspector Evans' office and said, "The boss wants us to interview Nathan Fawcett again."

CHAPTER THIRTY-FOUR

Nathan Fawcett was out on the forecourt speaking to a couple who were both dressed all in black. He spotted Keya and Nick's arrival in Keya's police car and ushered the couple across to the car showroom.

By the time Keya had parked and they had climbed out, Nathan had disappeared. But he soon reappeared when they walked towards the showroom.

"Officers," he greeted them over-brightly, his gaze flickering across to the display of cars and from one potential customer to another.

"I don't think you've been entirely truthful with us," announced Nick.

Nathan gulped.

"Your car, that is the company's courtesy car that you decided to drive on Friday afternoon, was spotted at the building site behind Akemans auction house around the time your sister died."

"I didn't kill her!" Nathan exclaimed and several potential customers turned in his direction. "I didn't," he pleaded in a quieter voice.

"But you were at the building site on Friday afternoon?" pressed Keya.

"Even though you made it appear that you were playing golf with Neil Cleavely at the Spring Hills Hotel," added Nick.

"You know all that?" Nathan's surprise was genuine.

"We do," confirmed Nick.

Keya's phone rang. It was Ryan.

"Excuse me," she said to Nick and Nathan.

As she answered the call, she heard Nick say, "You deliberately created a false alibi. That means ..."

"Hi," Keya answered her call and moved away so she couldn't be overheard.

"I think I've found a reason why Nathan Fawcett wouldn't be happy about his sister's re-appearance."

Keya's mouth felt dry, so she gulped before responding, "You have?"

"In Nathan's father's will, his estate was to be split equally between his children, Nathan and Rachael, and his wife. And while Rachael's whereabouts were unknown, Nathan was to manage and invest her share so it could grow. Then there are some figures and calculations but in effect, if Rachel's share from the pub sale was £100,000 thirty years ago, it would be worth at least £300,000 today in inflationary terms, and it could be argued from what've I've calculated, closer to £500,000."

"Are you saying Nathan owed Kate half a million pounds? But that would have kept her going for years. For life." Her initial surprise turned to confusion and Keya said, "But surely, she'd have been really excited about such a windfall. You met her in the pub. Do you think she acted like someone who'd come into a fortune?"

"No," admitted Ryan.

"Which makes me think she didn't know about it."

"Maybe she found out and confronted Nathan when they met on Friday," suggested Ryan.

"And they had a row, and he killed her. But he just vehemently denied doing so. Let me go and confront him with what you've just told me. Thanks."

Keya finished the call and returned to Nick and Nathan.

"We could charge you with perverting the course of justice," declared Nick as Nathan hung his head.

"I only did it because I didn't want people knowing I was meeting Rachael. She'd been pretending she was someone else for so long, who was I to blow her cover?"

"Is that really the reason?" asked Keya in a cynical tone.

"What do you mean?" Nathan frowned.

"It had nothing to do with the fact you owed her a share of your father's estate. Some half a million pounds in today's money."

The colour drained from Nathan's face. "I … I …" stammered Nathan.

"I think we should finish this interview down at the station," said Nick.

"I need to call my lawyer," protested Nathan.

"Good idea. You can make the call from the back of the squad car."

Nathan didn't move.

Nick sighed. "You can come willingly, or I can arrest and handcuff you."

"There's no need to do that." Beads of perspiration appeared on Nathan's forehead.

Back at Cirencester police station, Nick led Nathan to an interview room and left him while they waited for his lawyer to arrive.

"Bring me up to speed," grunted Inspector Evans as Nick joined him, Ryan, and Keya in the team room. "You have Nathan Fawcett in custody. Have you arrested him?"

"No," replied Nick. "He insists he didn't kill his sister but, as Ryan discovered, he's been hiding the fact that should she re-appear, he would owe her a share of their father's will."

"How much are we talking about?" asked the inspector.

"Around half a million pounds," confirmed Ryan.

The inspector whistled. "That's a lot of money, especially to us, but for a successful businessman like Nathan?"

"It could have ruined him," remarked Keya.

"How so?" The inspector narrowed his eyes at her.

She replied, "Ryan discovered he'd extended himself and

mortgaged his business premises and his house. And I have a contact who confirms this."

Ryan added, "But Keya's contact also thought that as long as nothing impacted his business, it was doing well enough to trade itself out of its current cash flow problems."

"But it wouldn't be able to do that if Nathan had to pay Kate what he owed her from the will," said Keya.

"It would bring the whole house of cards crashing down," emphasised Nick.

Keya was leaning against her desk, and she brought her hands in front of her and pressed her fingers together.

In a voice full of regret, she said, "But I don't think Kate knew anything about the money. She never mentioned it, and why would she be living in a small room above the pub if she had access to such funds?"

Keya tapped her fingertips together. "I think Kate was happy making her way. Sure, she'd have welcomed the money, who wouldn't? But I bet that if Nathan told her he was struggling at the moment, and asked would she mind waiting, I don't think she'd have objected. Maybe a few thousand pounds to help her out, but she'd waited thirty years, so what difference would a few more make? And wouldn't Nathan be better offering her a stake in his business since he's doing so well?"

Inspector Evans tilted his head back, staring up at the yellowing ceiling. "Those are all fair points, and if we could ask the deceased, I'm sure she'd be able to answer them. But as it is, she can't. To my mind, the inheritance puts Nathan squarely in the frame for his sister's murder." He stopped and stared at Nick and Keya. "Are you two happy to interview him, or shall I?"

Keya and Nick exchanged glances. Keya didn't want to hand over interviewing Nathan to the inspector, and she could see from Nick's determined expression, that neither did he.

Inspector Evans nodded in satisfaction. "We'll give him another fifteen minutes with his lawyer and then start your interview. We need him to admit that he owed Rachael the money, that he had difficulty paying it, and that they argued, and he killed her."

CHAPTER THIRTY-FIVE

Fifteen minutes later, Keya opened the door of interview room number two. A grey Formica table was pushed up against one of its grey walls and Nathan filled one of the black chairs facing the door. His equally well-proportioned lawyer, whose round glasses sat halfway down his nose, was next to him.

The lawyer peered imperiously over his glasses at Keya and Nick as they entered and sat down. Nick sat opposite the lawyer and Keya faced Nathan.

Nick tapped the recently upgraded recording equipment on the table, entering the date and time. Clicking record he stated, "Interview with Nathan Fawcett and his lawyer …". Nick looked at the man sitting opposite him.

The lawyer appeared to be weighing Nick up before he answered, "Giles Sefton."

The lawyer sounded pompous, and before Nick had a chance to open the questioning, he declared, "My client would like to make it clear that he had nothing to do with the death of the woman calling herself Katherine Dewsbury."

"You mean his sister, Rachael Fawcett?" stated Nick.

The lawyer looked at Nathan, who nodded his consent.

"My client confirms that she was indeed his sister Rachael, who went missing over thirty years ago, and was subsequently declared legally dead."

"But she could still claim her share of your father's will?" Keya blurted.

She ignored the look of annoyance Nick flashed her. He probably wanted to take the interview steadily and build up to the pertinent questions. Keya wanted answers now.

Nathan's shoulders sagged, and he gave a small nod.

Nick looked at the lawyer and said, "Can you confirm that Sergeant Varma's statement is correct?"

The lawyer didn't glance at his client but answered, "Yes."

Keya sat back and stared at Nathan. "But did she know anything about it? Did she ask you for money?"

Nathan clasped his hands together on the table. "I told you before, she never asked me for money."

"But did she know about the terms of the will?" repeated Nick.

Nathan shrugged his shoulders. "I don't know. I don't think so, but it was likely she would at some point. Her - what would you call him - stepfather, Brad, was sniffing around and asking questions."

Keya bit her lip, confused. Why would Brad be interested? It was the next question she asked. "Why was Bradley Dewsbury looking into the contents of your father's will?"

"Because he'd already come to me and asked for money. Said I was obviously doing well for myself and could afford to help my sister. I thought it was a sick joke and told him to get lost. But then he showed me photos of them together, of Rachael as she was, and then the woman she grew into. That was a shock, I can tell you."

Nathan paused and looked down at the table, appearing to gather his thoughts.

"I said I would be happy to help Rachael, but I wanted to meet her. To make sure she really was my sister, and find out why she disappeared and never got in touch."

"So what happened next?" asked Nick.

"Nothing for over a year. I thought it had been a hoax, and despite the photos, which had seemed real, I resigned myself to the fact Rachael was not alive. That Brad had been trying to con me. And then I saw her at the Spring Hills Hotel. My grown-up sister in the flesh."

He paused and looked at Keya before continuing, "To be honest, I panicked. I thought it was another way to get money out of me, so I avoided the hotel for a while."

"And then you bribed the manager to sack her," stated Ryan.

The lawyer raised his eyebrows. Clearly Nathan hadn't told him that.

Nathan hung his head in his hands.

"I'm not proud of that. It was a terrible thing to do. To anyone. Never mind my sister."

"So why did you do it?" demanded Keya. "And just before Christmas. She was lucky to get a job at my local pub when she didn't have a reference."

Nathan remained silent.

Nick crossed his arms. "I don't believe you. You knew she was Rachael. Which means you had another reason for wanting rid of her."

"Money," declared Keya, outraged. "You didn't want to pay her your father's share of the will. How selfish was that?"

"Very," agreed Nathan, not denying the accusation. "But I was about to open my new showroom in Cheltenham. People like me don't open upmarket car showrooms in places like Cheltenham. But it meant I didn't have the money to pay Rachael, and as I'm planning to expand the business to Gloucester, I didn't know when I would. So I mentioned to Neil that he might like to get rid of her."

"Mentioned? You paid him £2,000." Keya sat back and, mirroring Nick, crossed her arms.

Nick uncrossed his arms, and giving Keya a sympathetic look, he asked, "Did Rachael ever mention the will?"

Nathan's cheeks reddened in shame. "No, she didn't say a word about it."

"To be clear. Rachael never asked you about the will or the money from it. And she never asked you for any money."

Nathan sighed and looked across at his lawyer, who appeared to be struggling to keep up with the thread of the interview.

"And did Mr Dewsbury demand money from you again? And when was the last time you saw him?" Keya wondered if Nathan knew Brad was working at the building site at Akemans.

"Last year, and not since I met Rachael again."

"And you didn't see him on Friday?"

"Friday? Why would I have seen him then?"

"Because he was working on the building site," said Keya. "I saw him approach you in the morning."

"You mean that builder who chased me away was Bradley Dewsbury?" Nathan pulled at his ear in confusion. "But what was he doing there?"

"He works for the building company under the name Brad Daresbury."

"Did Rachael know that?"

"We don't know," admitted Nick.

"Why did you meet Rachael at Akemans?" asked Keya. "Why not your showroom?"

"I didn't want anywhere too public. And the river was where we spent our last happy moments together, the summer she disappeared."

"Did she tell you why she left?" Keya's voice was softer, but she hadn't forgiven Nathan for his treatment of his sister.

Nathan's voice was flat as he replied, "No, and that really hurt. I think it's why I felt justified in having her sacked from the Spring Hills. She left without telling me and all these years let me think that she'd been dead. I thought her disappearance was my fault. That I'd gone away with my mates and left her, rather than protecting her like an older brother should. I know my mum blamed me. We haven't spoken since she returned to Wales. So when I saw Rachael again, and she still refused to tell me why she'd left, I was hurt. And angry."

Giles Sefton looked at his watch before clearing his throat. "My client has answered all your questions, and it's clear he had nothing to do with Katherine Dewsbury's death."

"It isn't," bridled Nick. "He hasn't told us what happened when he met her on Friday morning, and why he created a false alibi to meet her again on Friday afternoon."

"Or how he contacted her," said Keya, her eyes narrowing as they fixed on Nathan. "Did you know your sister was working at the Dog and Duck pub?"

Nathan puffed out his cheeks. "It was my duty to keep an eye on Rachael."

Keya continued to stare at Nathan. "You knew she was seeing one of your staff, didn't you? Is that how you got hold of her telephone number? Did you call her and arrange to meet her on Friday morning?"

"OK, OK. I did find her number on Wayne's phone, when my PA distracted him one day. But why shouldn't I want to get in touch with my sister?"

Nick placed his hands on the table and in a calm voice said, "You called Rachael and arranged to meet her. Why?"

"I'd heard Wayne talking about her. He might come across as a bit of a thug, but he really felt something for my sister. Would you believe me if I said I missed her?"

"Maybe," muttered Keya, continuing to stare at Nathan.

"So you met up on the riverbank behind Akemans on Friday morning," stated Nick.

"Yes, but just briefly so I could give her the money. That builder chased us away, so I sent her a message begging her to come back in the afternoon. That I really needed to speak with her."

"After you tried to bribe her?" stated Keya.

Nathan sniffed, and his eyes glistened. "She was so grateful for the money and insisted I didn't have to give her anything, that she would sort herself out, as she always had. But I knew she had nowhere to live, but she made me feel guilty. Here I was giving her a fraction of what I owed her, and she was trying to push it back to me, as if I was the one who needed it."

"For your business," muttered Keya sarcastically.

Nick ignored her and asked, "But did she take it?"

"Yes. I told her to rent herself a nice apartment or a small house, and that when things were less busy with work, I'd come and visit her." A tear slipped down his cheek. "She smiled and said she'd like that. That she wanted to settle down. But then she became serious and said that before she did, she had to make right something terrible that she'd done. I asked what it was, but she shook her head and refused to tell me."

Nathan shook his own head. "I should have pressed her and made her tell me. I could have helped her."

"Yes, you could," snapped Keya. "So why didn't you?" She was annoyed with Nathan again.

"I was so relieved that she took the money without question, and that we were friends again, that I didn't want to ruin it."

"You didn't want to know, more likely," spat Keya.

Nathan hung his head in shame again. "You're right. I didn't."

"Then what happened?" asked Nick.

"I walked away and left her. On the side of the river. It was the last time I saw her. Just like thirty-one years ago."

"Did you see anyone else?"

"No," sighed Nathan wearily. "I got in my car, reversed carefully so as to avoid a vintage motorbike, and left Rachael staring into the water."

CHAPTER THIRTY-SIX

Keya and Nick left Nathan and his protesting lawyer in the interview room at Cirencester police station and went in search of Inspector Evans. He was in the team room, staring at the printer positioned beside the partition wall of his office. The printer whirled and a coloured sheet slowly emerged.

The inspector grabbed it, and staring hard, asked, "Are you sure this photo was taken on the Thursday Rachael was seen cycling through Coln Akeman?"

"Yes, I checked with the local newspaper. They ran it the next day," confirmed Ryan, looking up from his desk.

"Then Nathan didn't kill Katherine Dewsbury, the child." The inspector turned his attention to Keya and Nick. "But did he kill the modern-day version?"

"According to the evidence, he could have," Keya agreed reluctantly, even though she wasn't certain he had. "He was at the scene at the right time. He purposefully created a false alibi, and he had a strong motive. Money."

"Sergeant Unwin?" asked the inspector.

"That's all true, but where is the money he said he was giving Kate, and where is the murder weapon?" Nick replied.

"We only have his word there was any money, and he could have found something on the building site or lying around at Akemans to hit her with. It would be easy enough to dispose of the murder weapon in the river," considered Inspector Evans, "but I can see that neither of you is totally convinced he's our man. And if we think the same person killed the girl and the woman, then it can't be Nathan."

"Why?" asked Keya.

"Because of this photo young Ryan found." Inspector Evans handed Keya the printed sheet of a blurry photograph of a group of young people enjoying themselves. "It was taken the day Rachael disappeared."

Nick coughed. "Nathan's lawyer is making a fuss about still being here. What shall we do?"

Inspector Evans pondered the question for a minute or so before replying. "I don't think he's a flight risk, and we know where he lives and works. Let him go, but tell him and his lawyer we're not totally satisfied with his story and may have further questions for him."

As Nick left to sort out Nathan Fawcett, the phone on his desk rang.

Inspector Evans stared at it and instructed, "Answer that, Sergeant Varma."

Keya picked up the phone. "Sergeant Unwin's phone. This is Sergeant Varma speaking."

"Oh, hello. This is Tim Simmonds. I have a message to call your colleague."

"Did he speak to you yesterday?"

"No, I was down in Devon on a delivery. Which is why I'm phoning now."

Keya remembered that Tim had been working at Akemans when Katherine was killed, but he still thought it was Rachael. Would that make a difference to the events he remembered? She decided to take a chance.

"Are you somewhere private?" she asked.

"I can be, just a minute." She thought she heard a vehicle door open, some deeper breathing, and then the outside world was cut off as a door closed. "I'm inside one of my lorry cabs," explained Tim.

"What I'm about to tell you isn't public knowledge, so please keep it to yourself," instructed Keya.

"OK," replied Tim warily.

"The remains that we found at Akemans weren't those of Rachael Fawcett," stated Keya.

"What? Do you mean Rachael is alive?" Tim sounded surprised and hopeful.

"She was until someone killed her last Friday."

"What?" repeated Tim. "Do you mean the body found at Akemans wasn't Katherine Dewsbury's? Why does everyone think it is? I don't understand."

"It is rather complex and has taken some unravelling." Keya explained about Rachael taking Katherine's identity and moving to Scotland. She then asked, "If you'd known Katherine had been killed and Rachael was alive, but with Mr Dewsbury, would that have made a difference to your statement thirty-one years ago?"

There was silence on the other end of the phone.

"Katherine was a quiet kid. I could tell she loved playing with Rachael and Gilly, who could both be quite naughty, but she was always the last to join in. I think she was afraid of her father. He was so domineering. I remember once he caught me talking to the girls. I think they were trying to get me to give them something, like a rope or a hammer and nails. Anyway, Mr Dewsbury started shouting and swearing at me and telling me to leave his daughter alone. I could see by the way she shrank back that she was scared of him."

Then Tim laughed, which wasn't what Keya was expecting. "Rachael was the only one who wasn't. She stood up to Katherine's father and I can tell you, he didn't like that. He didn't know what to do."

"Did you ever see Mr Dewsbury hit his daughter?" asked Keya.

"No, but it wouldn't surprise me if he did. Hey, but now I come to think of it, there was some kerfuffle concerning Rachael. She broke her finger but refused to tell her parents how. But one of the men staying in the pub had seen her and Mr Dewsbury arguing. I think Rachael's father confronted Mr Dewsbury, but I don't know what the outcome was."

"And when did you last see Mr Dewsbury?"

"Well that's the funny thing. Everyone said he and his daughter left the day before Rachael disappeared. I went along with it but actually, now I think about it, I thought I saw him and a young girl, who I presumed was Katherine, drive past Akemans in an old van the morning before I found the bicycle."

"That would be Thursday morning, the day Rachael was reported missing, after she was seen riding her bicycle through Coln Akeman."

"Yes," agreed Tim.

Keya tapped her fingers on Nick's desk.

"Is that all?" asked Tim.

"Do you remember the girl with Mr Dewsbury in the van? Could it have been Rachael rather than Katherine?" asked Keya.

"I really couldn't say. I just have the impression of an upset young girl."

If it was Rachael, when had Katherine died?

"When was the last time you saw Katherine?" Keya asked.

"That would have been a couple of days before. She and Rachael were swimming and messing about by the river. Gilly wasn't there, as she and George had gone away with their mum. I think it was one of the last really hot days. Rachael's brother and his friends joined them, and they were drinking. I remember wishing I could stop work for a cold beer. I was helping Mr Dewsbury cut down a tree and I could see him becoming more and more angry at the antics by the river.

"Eventually he left me cutting up wood with a chainsaw and stormed over to the group. I couldn't hear or see much as I was concentrating on my work, but when I finished, I heard Rachael shouting, and then her brother and his friends stormed off. I'm not sure what happened after that. I think I had to go help my dad."

"That's really useful, thank you," said Keya. "We may need a formal statement from you later."

"No problem, but I'm driving to Burnley tonight and won't be back until late tomorrow."

Keya put Nick's phone down and jumped when Nick asked, "Who was that?"

"Tim Simmonds. Did you leave him a message to call you?"

"Yes, he was away when I visited his delivery business yesterday. But I didn't think Katherine's death thirty-one years ago was our priority."

"It is if the two deaths are connected, and I still think they are." Keya recounted her conversation with Tim Simmonds.

"So you believe," surmised Nick, "that Brad Dewsbury, or Daresbury as he now calls himself, is the link between the two deaths?"

"I hadn't thought of it like that, but yes, I guess you're right," agreed Keya.

"Then let's go and speak to him," Nick replied.

CHAPTER THIRTY-SEVEN

Once again, Keya drove Nick in her police car, this time to Akemans.

"Hi, Keya," greeted Gilly as they walked across the gravel car park in front of the antiques centre. "I see Rowan's getting on with removing the waterwheel. His group have been very busy erecting scaffolding around the wheel and cutting off the paddles."

"That is good news." Keya was about to walk on, as she didn't want to be distracted by the cafe building work at the moment, but then she stopped and turned back to Gilly. She asked, "Do you remember an incident when Rachael broke her finger?"

"Gosh, yes, I do. That was a nasty business, but Rachael was so brave. I don't think it ever healed straight. We were messing around at the back of the old mill, the part which hadn't been converted into the antiques centre, and Mr Dewsbury spotted us and started chasing us. I've no idea why he didn't want us inside. He probably thought it was dangerous and Katherine would fall. I'm not sure what happened, but we were trying to hide from him when Rachael's finger got caught in a piece of old equipment. I don't think Mr Dewsbury realised, as he grabbed the piece to move it out of the way and Rachel's finger …"

Gilly shivered.

Keya continued, "Was that the only time he hurt any of you? Did he hit or abuse Katherine?"

Gilly pinched her lips together. Then she said, "I don't think so, but I can't be certain. He was very protective of her, and he did have a temper."

"Have you seen him recently?" asked Nick.

"Mr Dewsbury!" exclaimed Gilly. "Not for over thirty years. Why, should I have?"

Nick and Keya exchanged glances.

"We heard he might be back in the area," replied Keya limply.

"He'll be an old man, now. I doubt I'd recognise him. Anyway, I must go. I'm helping George with the auction. You're still helping out next Wednesday and Thursday, aren't you?" Gilly asked Keya.

"As long as these cases are wrapped up. But if they're not, I think we'll have run out of leads." Keya and Nick walked round the side of Akemans while Gilly bustled back to the antiques centre.

"You've met Brad Daresbury, haven't you?" said Nick. "What do you think of him?"

"He seems very unassuming, hardworking, and pleasant. And he gets on with whatever Vic tasks him with, without complaint."

"He's a very different character from the Bradley Dewsbury people have spoken about thirty-one years ago. What if he isn't our man?" asked Nick.

"Then I guess we'll have to keep looking."

They walked around the end of the auction building and past a vintage motorbike with a black leather seat and loads of gleaming chrome. The registration number was printed on a plaque above the front wheel. Nick stopped and went back to examine it.

"This is a Triumph from the 1950s," he said. "It's been very well maintained."

A voice called, "There's nothing wrong, is there, Officer?"

Keya turned round and, organising her face into a pleasant expression, said, "Hi, Brad. My colleague was just admiring this bike. Is it yours?" She remembered the bowling-ball shaped helmet she'd seen him carrying, the one he'd moved out of her way so she could reach the mugs at the site meeting.

"Yes," he replied, shifting from foot to foot.

"Very nice," agreed Nick, joining them. "I'm glad we found you. We have a few questions."

Brad glanced at the motorbike.

He wasn't considering making a hasty escape, was he? Keya stepped to one side, blocking his route to the motorbike.

"I think we'll do this down at the station," Nick stated.

"Why? Are you arresting me? What have I done?" cried Brad.

Nick's voice remained calm as he replied, "No, we're not arresting you. But we do need to ask you some questions and I think it best we do so in a proper interview environment, rather than the edge of a building site."

Keya heard an electric saw, and she stared across at the waterwheel. Several figures were moving around it, some at a higher level, on what she assumed was scaffolding.

"I don't want to go." Brad sounded petulant, and he crossed his arms.

"There's no need to make this difficult." Nick sounded bored. "But I can handcuff you if you refuse to come willingly."

Brad gulped and glanced around. "But my work?"

"Keya, Sergeant Varma, will explain to the foreman that you're helping us. After all, you were the last person on the site on Friday, so it's only reasonable we should want to interview you."

Nick's statement seemed to calm Brad.

"All right. I'll come. But you have to drop me back here afterwards to collect my bike. I don't like leaving it outside overnight."

Keya handed Nick her car keys, and he took Brad by the arm and turned back towards the car park. She entered the building site, trying to work out what Rowan and his team were doing while she negotiated the planks across the bare earth.

She stopped beside the extension. The final wall of the foundations was complete and within the area they marked out, a cement mixer was churning. Wooden planks laid out on their sides formed rectangles. One was already full of drying concrete, and it looked as if another was ready to be filled.

She found Vic in his office.

"Checking on our progress?" asked Vic, grinning.

"No, we've come to ask Brad some questions since he closed up the site on Friday. But we need a formal statement, so we're taking him to the station."

Vic checked his watch. "Then I doubt he'll be back to lock up. I'll do that tonight. Thanks for letting me know."

Keya nodded.

"And Rowan and his gang should be finished tomorrow, so we'll be starting on the exterior wall. It's all starting to come together," announced Vic proudly.

"Yes, I saw you've started on the floor slab for the extension."

Keya was walking out of the building when Vic shouted. "You better take Brad's motorcycle helmet. He'll need it later."

Keya retraced her steps and picked up the smooth, round, maroon-coloured helmet, and headed back to her car.

CHAPTER THIRTY-EIGHT

Nick led Brad into an interview room and said, "You've not been arrested, but we will be formally questioning you. Would you like to phone a lawyer?"

Hovering in the doorway, Keya heard Brad reply, "I don't know any …" Keya winced at his choice of language, " … lawyers."

Nick did well to maintain a calm and casual approach as he suggested, "Would you like me to contact the duty solicitor?"

"How much will that cost me?" sneered Brad.

"It's pro-bono, which means it's free, but there's unlikely to be anyone available for a few hours."

Keya checked her watch. It was half past three. She remembered she was supposed to be at Zivah's second dress fitting in Cheltenham at five. That looked unlikely unless Brad calmed down and answered their questions quickly and truthfully.

"I'm not sitting here waiting for some toffee-nosed lawyer," grunted Brad.

Inspector Evans poked his head out of the team room. Keya walked towards him as he asked, "What's going on?"

"Brad Daresbury, or Dewsbury, looked as if he might do a runner, so Nick decided we should bring him back to the station for his interview."

"He doesn't seem very happy about it. What's the shouting for?"

"He's declining the offer of a lawyer."

"Is that it? Well if things turn nasty, call me, but first try to calm Mr Daresbury down."

Keya left Inspector Evans and entered the interview room as Nick said, "Also present, Sergeant Varma."

Keya smiled at Brad, trying to set him at ease.

"Thank you for agreeing to be interviewed, Mr Daresbury, or is it Dewsbury?" Nick's opening question appeared to have delivered a punch to Brad's gut as he folded an arm across his stomach. He was also temporarily speechless.

Eventually he said, in a despondent voice, "So you know about that?"

Keya decided to take advantage of a less confrontational Brad and replied, "We do, and Kate. We're sorry for your loss. It must have been a terrible shock arriving at work on Friday morning and finding that the girl you'd raised had been killed."

"Och, it was," he replied, reverting to Scottish vocabulary.

But Nick was clearly not treading gently as he asked, "But she wasn't actually your daughter, was she?"

"I don't know what you mean," spluttered Brad.

"We know from her DNA that she was really Rachael Fawcett, the young girl who everyone thought had gone missing thirty-one years ago," Keya explained, slowly and steadily, trying to keep the interview on even footing.

Brad's eyes bulged in shock.

Keya was concerned that Brad might have a seizure or worse, as he was not a spring chicken. "I knew Kate," she said gently. "She worked at my local pub, and she was a lovely woman."

"She was," agreed Brad in a small voice, "but headstrong and wayward. She should never have left home." Brad closed his eyes and massaged his forehead. "Katherine was led astray by those two friends of hers. I kept warning her she'd land herself in trouble. And then there were the boys. Older boys with cars, loud music, and alcohol. Dangerous boys."

Nick and Keya looked at each other. Nick was clearly confused, but Keya thought she understood. Brad was mixing up the past and the present. Mixing up his daughter and Rachael, or Kate as she became.

"Tell me about Katherine," suggested Keya in a gentle voice. "Someone described her as angelic."

Brad's face softened. "She was, with her sweet smile and blonde hair. My little girl."

Nick almost succeeded in keeping the sarcastic edge out of his voice as he stated, "But young girls grow up into women."

Brad seemed to ignore the tone as he shook his head. "Not my Katherine."

Nick was about to speak again, but Keya placed a hand on his arm and shook her head. She might not be the best interviewer, but she could recognise when a softer touch was needed. She sensed that while Brad was reminiscing, he could actually be blurring the boundaries between past and present, and careful questioning might lead to the truth about Katherine, the girl.

"Why's that? Where's your Katherine?" asked Keya softly.

"She's with the angels." Brad looked up at her, a sincere expression on his face.

Nick coughed, possibly to cover a laugh of incredulity.

"I'm pleased she's at peace. When did she go there?"

"Go?" Brad asked sharply.

Keya was concerned she was losing her opportunity. "When did sweet Katherine join the angels?" She kept her tone gentle and level.

"It was a long time ago." Brad looked down at his hands with a sad expression.

This was the tricky part. Keya needed Brad to tell her what had happened, but in asking she might shock him back into the present and he'd return to his defensive, angry side. "Something happened to Katherine, didn't it? Did she float away?"

"Not on the river, no. She fell the other side, where it was dry. But I covered her up and left her in peace."

Keya felt Nick tense, but continued, "She'd have liked that. As if she was sleeping."

Brad nodded.

"Did Rachael leave her flowers?"

It was a question too far.

Brad snarled. "That little minx. It was all her fault. It was her brother and his friends corrupting my daughter. I had to protect Katherine. I had to take her away, but she wouldn't let me. That Rachael stood between us and shouted at me to leave Katherine alone. Who was she to tell me what to do, and with my own daughter?" snarled Brad.

Again Nick was about to speak, but Keya placed a restraining hand on his arm. She could see Brad was about to speak again and this time she felt the floodgates would open.

"I pushed her out of the way, but she swayed on the wall. I swung my hoe at her, but she swayed again, and Katherine stepped closer to steady her. Katherine, my angel, who never did anyone any harm. The hoe hit her and she fell. Rachel was shouting at me. Shouting at Katherine. She jumped into the channel, and I watched as she held Katherine's head. Her tears mingled with mine as my sweet daughter died."

CHAPTER THIRTY-NINE

Nick and Keya both took deep breaths after Brad's confession of how he'd killed his daughter, Katherine.

Nick looked at Keya for the lead, so she said, "I'm so very sorry. You must have been very upset. But didn't you think Katherine deserved a proper burial, and a funeral."

Brad bridled. "Why? Who would mourn her more than me? She was in her own special place. Where I heard her laugh and sing that summer. Why move her?"

"And Rachael?" asked Keya, not knowing what reaction Brad would have to her name.

"It was all her fault," he spat. "She was the reason my daughter was dead. And I told her so. Said that if the police knew what she'd done, she'd be sent to prison FOR LIFE. That scared her, I can tell you."

"Is that why she agreed to move to Scotland with you?" pressed Keya.

"I told her she had to take Katherine's place so nobody would know what had happened. I slept in the van so everyone would think Katherine and I had left, and the next day, Rachael rode her bicycle through the village. I picked her up on the road to Akemans and we left the bicycle."

"And you and Rachael moved to Inverness?"

"Yes, although she was too headstrong to be my Katherine. And then she grew up and left." Brad fixed a cunning look on Keya, and she knew he was firmly back in the present. She looked at Nick and inclined her head.

Nick asked, "When the mill closed, why did you decide to move back to the Cotswolds?"

"Cause it was where I was from," replied Brad defensively.

"And when did you decide to search for Kate?" Nick probed.

"I didn't." Brad looked from Nick's set impression to Keya's unbelieving one. "I needed money after the mill closed," he admitted, his shoulders slumping.

"And where did you find her?"

"I didn't to start with. I knew she moved around, and I thought I was wrong and she hadn't come back here. But then I saw her when the company was doing some repair work at a hotel."

"And did you ask her for money?" pressed Nick.

Brad hung his head. "Yes. I'd started working for the building company, but I wanted a place of my own. Nowhere big or posh. Just somewhere for me and my bike. Kate was living at the hotel, and she earned a decent wage. And she told me she'd been saving up her tips. I begged her to lend me that money. It was enough for a deposit to rent a small place in Cirencester."

"Did you ever pay her back?" probed Keya.

Brad hung his head, and muttered, "I meant to."

Keya didn't believe him and then she remembered her interviews with Nathan. "When you couldn't find Kate, after you moved down to the Cotswolds, did you speak to Nathan Fawcett? Did you tell him his sister was alive, and ask him for money?"

"I might have," murmured Brad, looking across the room.

"But he wouldn't give you any, unless you could prove Rachael was alive."

"Erm," was the unsatisfactory response Brad gave Keya.

"But then Nathan also met Kate at the Spring Hills Hotel and they recognised each other as siblings. You had no leverage then. No way to get any money from Nathan."

"I didn't need it," protested Brad. "I actually enjoy working for Vic and the pay's improved."

Keya mused, "So you left Nathan and Kate alone, until they both turned up at your building site at Akemans."

Brad sat back. His eyes were alert and flitted between Keya and Nick.

Keya wasn't sure if Brad had continued to pester Kate or Nathan for money, but she wanted to know what had happened the day Kate died, so she said, "Vic sent you to speak to Nathan and Kate for trespassing on the building site. You recognised them, didn't you? And did they know who you were?"

Brad shrugged.

Keya continued, "But they left after seeing you. Did you know they'd arranged to meet back at the site in the afternoon, or was it a surprise when they turned up as you were tidying up?"

Keya remembered what Wayne had said about Kate needing to right wrongs, and she'd told Nathan she had to make right something terrible she'd done. "Or did Kate come looking for you? To confront you about the day Katherine died?"

Brad crossed his arms and clamped his lips together.

Nick asked, "Was it like thirty-one years ago? But this time you hit Rachael, and she fell into the trench. What did you hit her with?"

Brad narrowed his eyes, staring at Nick.

"I know," squawked Keya. She remembered Brad's motorcycle helmet, which she'd carried in from the car and left beside her chair. She leaned down, picked it up, and placed it on the table. Staring at it she commented, "It's a useful colour to hide blood, but if there is any trace, we'll find it."

Nick moved the helmet towards him and considered the rim of metal which ran around it. "And we might be able to match the DNA of the hair caught on it."

"All right. All right. I did hit her."

Keya and Nick stared at Brad but remained silent.

"She was doing it again. Standing at the back of Akemans just like last time, defying me." Brad blinked and Keya felt the shift in his personality. His voice was almost childlike as he said, "She told me Katherine had been found. And her body disturbed and removed. And now it was time to finally tell the truth. But what truth? My darling daughter is dead." And then Brad burst into large, heart-racking tears.

Nick stated, "Interview terminated at 4.40."

Keya jumped up and cried, "I have to go."

Keya drove her police car and parked on the single yellow line outside Laboni's dress shop in Cheltenham, deciding that her sister's anger over her being any later outweighed any irritation she'd have about Keya's car.

She rushed inside gasping, "Sorry I'm late." It was a quarter past five.

"Better than last time," mused Zivah as she turned to face Keya.

Keya gasped. Zivah wasn't wearing a traditional brightly coloured wedding dress, but a wonderfully ornate ivory lehangas. The heavily gold embroidered top was cropped, revealing Zivah's narrow waist. It was both modern and daring and not what Keya had been expecting. But she loved the richness and detailing of the embroidery on the floor length skirt. "You look beautiful."

Zivah's face softened and there was a tear in her eye as she held her arms out to Keya and they hugged. "Do you think it's OK?"

"I think it's perfect."

As Keya was toasting Zivah with a glass of sparkling elderflower, her phone rang. Looking at the display, she excused herself.

"Hi, Nick, has something happened?" she asked when she answered the call.

"No. Brad wouldn't say anything else, so he's been taken for processing. I've asked the duty nurse to give him a thorough examination as we don't want anything to happen to him overnight."

"Good idea," replied Keya.

"And I've spoken to Nathan and explained he's no longer a suspect, but we do need to formally interview him again, but as a witness."

"How did he respond to that?"

"With an air of self-importance. Said he'd be delighted to help the police, and he doesn't need the assistance of an expensive lawyer."

"That's a bonus," agreed Keya.

"I think you should be there, but you're supposed to be speaking at a Primary School. I've suggested that Ryan stand in for you."

"Really? What did he say?"

"Ryan? He was lost for words, but the inspector said it was a good idea and suggested Ryan speak about being open and honest, and tells the children that if they see or do something they know is wrong, they should tell someone. Even if they get into trouble, it's better than hiding it until later, as the truth always comes out."

"That sounds a fun talk," Keya said sarcastically. "Poor Ryan."

"Don't worry. I suggested he take his laptop and a projector and show the children how to access different databases, or take their fingerprints and search for matches."

Keya laughed. "Those sound like much better suggestions. I usually talk about road safety or stranger danger. Maybe I should take Ryan with me next time for some practical demonstrations."

"Nathan agreed to come to the station for half past eight. Is that OK?"

"Sure, I'll see you tomorrow."

CHAPTER FORTY

Keya and Nick sat in the grey-walled interview room the following morning, facing Nathan Fawcett.

Nathan opened with, "If I'm no longer a suspect, I presume you've found whoever killed my sister?"

Nick and Keya looked at each other. They'd discussed their response to this question with Inspector Evans before the interview started, and had decided to tell Nathan the whole truth.

Nick said, "Brad Daresbury, formally known as Bradley Dewsbury, has confessed to killing the woman known as Kate Dewsbury last Friday night. And Kate was your sister, Rachael."

Keya added, "He also confessed to killing his daughter thirty-one years ago."

Nathan leaned forward. "Did he confess to kidnapping Rachael?"

"Not exactly," admitted Keya. "But from what he did say, it's clear he coerced her into leaving with him by telling her she would be blamed for Katherine's death."

"But Rachael didn't kill her, did she?" gasped Nathan.

"No," reassured Keya. "She was standing up for Katherine, and she was the one Mr Dewsbury was aiming at. But Katherine stepped into the way and took a blow to the head. But I think Mr Dewsbury made

Rachael feel the full guilt of Katherine's death, telling her she was the one who should be dead. I've no idea how that affected your sister, but it's not surprising that, after what happened, she didn't settle at school, and she spent her adult life moving from one place to another."

"Poor Rachael. But why kill her now? After all this time. He could have done it in Scotland, and nobody would have known."

Which Keya knew wasn't true, especially in a small Scottish community where everyone knew everyone else's business, but she understood what Nathan meant, so she said, "Discovering Katherine's body was probably the catalyst. We're not sure if Mr Dewsbury is showing the first signs of dementia. That will need a medical diagnosis, but he did come across as living part of his life in the past.

"Whether he did so before the skeleton was found, we've no idea, but finding it on the site he was working on, and then seeing Kate, the older version of your sister, Rachael, was too much. And we know Kate wanted to 'right wrongs' and probably reveal what happened and how Katherine died. It was too much for Mr Dewsbury. We think he swung at her with his motorcycle helmet."

Nathan leaned back and stared up at the ceiling. "I should never have left Kate alone at Akemans on Friday. But I was in a rush to get back to the showroom before closing and she insisted she had something to do. I thought she just wanted to revisit her childhood haunts, or visit the place where the skeleton had been found. I had no idea it would lead to her death."

He took a deep breath and then asked, "Have you found the money?"

Keya bit her lip. That was a good point.

"We're still processing her possessions," Nick responded swiftly.

Nathan looked about to say something else but clamped his mouth shut.

Had he been about to ask for the money back? Keya felt her face redden, but she breathed deeply to calm herself down.

They asked Nathan a few more questions, but it was clear he had nothing useful to tell them.

When he'd left, Nick explained, "I've arranged a duty solicitor for Brad, since we can't be certain of his medical condition. I'll see if they've arrived."

Nick returned with a young woman with wavy brown hair and a grey suit that was slightly too large for her.

During their second interview with Brad, the solicitor said very little, but that was hardly surprising as her client clammed up and refused to say anything.

When they realised they were making absolutely no progress, they ended the interview and Nick escorted Brad back to his holding cell.

Keya thanked the duty solicitor before making teas and coffees for herself, Nick and Inspector Evans. She had just handed them out in the team room when a beaming Ryan appeared in the doorway.

"I take it that was a success, Constable?" Inspector Evans said in an ironic tone.

"It was great fun. We took fingerprints with the new mobile machine and compared them with ink copies. And the kids cried out in delight when their teacher's much younger face appeared on the screen after I used his fingerprints to search for him on our system. Apparently, he was once arrested for protesting against experiments on animals. He was rather proud of it."

"Good job, and what about you two?" asked the inspector.

Nick answered. "Brad Daresbury wouldn't say anything, but Nathan was very talkative. Not that he had much to say except that he left Kate at Akemans."

Inspector Evans strode over to the two boards and stuck the women's names back on them. "So we're confident Bradley Dewsbury, now known as Daresbury, killed both victims?"

"Yes," chorused Nick and Keya together.

"I sent the motorcycle helmet to the lab in Gloucester, but we won't get a result until next week," cautioned Ryan.

"If we're happy we have our man, we can start the legal process," stated the inspector. "Although the duty nurse has recommended a full medical examination. That's taking place this afternoon."

Keya had plenty of paperwork to catch up on, and so it seemed did Nick and Ryan.

They were all working quietly at their desks when Ryan's phone rang.

He groaned before answering it. Keya heard Ozzie Winters shout, "When were you going to tell me the identities of the bodies were the wrong way round? And is it true you've arrested someone for their deaths?"

Inspector Evans stepped out of his office and, staring at the incident boards, muttered, "This place leaks like a sieve."

CHAPTER FORTY-ONE

Keya wasn't surprised to receive an invitation to supper at Meadowbank Farm on Saturday night. Aunt Beanie liked to keep abreast of news and events from the police station and, with the builders' recent discovery of a second skeleton inside the antiques centre at Akemans, there was much to tell.

Keya entered the farmhouse kitchen carrying a large, oval, metal container planted with purple pansies, white calla lilies, and other colourful flowers she didn't know the names of.

"How lovely," exclaimed Aunt Beanie. "I'll put it outside the front door to welcome future visitors."

Marmaduke, Gilly and Dr Peter Wimsey, Ryan, and Ozzie were already sitting at the pine kitchen table chatting to Norman, Akemans' porter and Aunt Beanie's lodger.

"Is Nick joining us?" asked Keya tentatively.

"No," replied Aunt Beanie curtly as she carried the container of flowers out of the kitchen.

Norman looked up and remarked, "She hasn't forgiven him for his behaviour towards Dotty."

Keya sat down opposite Ozzie, between Ryan and Dr Peter, as Aunt Beanie returned to the kitchen and joined them. She sat down and said, "Please can you pass the wine, Peter?"

Holding the bottle, Aunt Beanie fixed her gaze on Keya and said, "Ryan has refused to tell us any more about the second skeleton the builders found at Akemans. He insisted we wait for you."

"Has it really been hidden away in the wall in the antiques centre since Dad built the original toilets and storerooms?" blurted Gilly.

"It had nothing to do with me," declared Marmaduke. "I swear we didn't hide a person, or a body, when we undertook the original renovation work."

"But I'm afraid someone did," replied Keya.

"But what about the smell?" enquired Norman.

"Rats," announced Marmaduke as he lifted his tumbler to his lips and took a slug of whisky.

"We had a huge problem with them," explained Aunt Beanie. "And poisoned ones kept dying in the walls and under the floor, creating awful smells. Besides, we didn't use the mill space all the time, only for additional sales of auction items."

"So whose is the body?" asked Ozzie, leaning forward.

Keya bit her lip before replying, "Her name won't be officially announced until tomorrow."

"I promise I won't print anything until it is," assured Ozzie.

"We found the remains of a wallet with the body and a bank card in the name of Elizabeth Dewsbury," announced Keya.

"Katherine's mum," cried Gilly.

"I never believed she ran away with a soldier," cited Aunt Beanie before pouring red wine into her glass.

"And SOCO have confirmed her DNA matches her records, and that she is a close match to the DNA of the skeleton of the child, which ties it all together."

"Poor Katherine," moaned Gilly.

"I presume Brad Dewsbury is the culprit." said Ozzie. "And that he killed his wife and to cover it up, told everyone she had run away to Germany with a solider."

"We believe so, but we haven't been able to ask him any more questions since he was placed in a remand hospital. The doctor thinks the stress of recent events has accelerated the onset of his dementia," explained Keya.

"But we do think he did it," added Ryan.

Dr Peter laid his hands on the table and said, "It's a sad story but I, for one, am pleased it's finally been laid to rest."

Everyone around the table nodded in agreement.

Ozzie peered at Keya and asked, "But what about the money? Ryan told me Nathan Fawcett gave some money to Kate before she was killed, but he's refused to tell me where it went." Ozzie turned accusatory eyes on Ryan, whose cheeks and ears flushed pink.

"We can't tell you everything about a case, can we, Keya?" implored Ryan.

"But if I promise not to report it?" appealed Ozzie.

"I'd like to know about the money," added Aunt Beanie. "I can sense an interesting story. Is it one with a happy ending?"

Keya sighed and smiled. "It is. And all thanks to Ryan."

Ryan turned scarlet as everyone seated around the table stared at him. "You tell them," he muttered to Keya.

"For some reason, Ryan took it upon himself to start meeting and giving life advice to Kate's ex-boyfriend, the rough-around-the-edges Wayne Hourigan."

"Why would you want to do that?" demanded Ozzie.

"He needed someone to talk to," reasoned Ryan. "And I doubt he could open up to his mates at work or in the pub."

Ozzie rolled her eyes.

"Ryan arranged to meet Wayne at Joe's cafe for Sunday brunch. But we still had all of Kate's clothes and her car. Of course, Nathan, as her next of kin, was keen to have her Mini, but he wasn't interested in her possessions and told us to send them to a charity shop.

"When Ryan told Wayne this, he asked if he could have something to remember her by, and he told us about a music box, with a ballerina, in which she kept some cheap jewellery. We found the box in her suitcase and when Ryan and Wayne met a second time, he handed over the music box. And can you believe what was stuffed inside?"

"The money," stated Aunt Beanie with satisfaction.

"All £10,000 of it," revealed Keya.

"So that made my discussion with Wayne much easier," confided Ryan. "We agreed he would use the money to buy a flight to Africa."

"And is that where he's gone?" asked Gilly.

"It is," confirmed Keya, "to work with a charity in Malawi."

"That is a happy ending," agreed Aunt Beanie.

"And I still might get a story out of it," mused Ozzie. "Forty-year-old mechanic loses girlfriend and takes up charity work in Africa. But I need a better title."

Nobody offered her one.

Aunt Beanie broke the silence by asking, "Has anyone heard from Dotty this week?"

"No," everyone murmured in response.

Ryan cleared his throat and asked, "I was wondering. Would it be possible to stay in Dotty's cottage? Just until she returns, or I find a place of my own."

"That's just what I've been saying," agreed Norman. "I told Beanie it wasn't easy for you back at your parents' place, and you could help Dotty out by paying some of the rent."

"Do you think she would mind?" asked Ryan.

"Why don't we ask her?" beamed Aunt Beanie. "It would be fantastic to talk to her while everyone is here." She stood up and collected a tablet, which she passed to Ryan. "You're better at this type of thing than me."

After several electronic rings, Dotty's face appeared on the screen. She was holding her British blue cat, Earl Grey. "Hi Ryan, I wasn't expecting to see you."

Keya leaned towards Ryan until her face also appeared in the rectangular box at the top of the screen. "Hiya," she called. "You won't believe this!"

"What?" asked Dotty, stroking Earl Grey.

"We only managed to solve a murder case without you."

Dotty laughed.

"And it was a complex one," added Ryan.

"Well done, and I can happily say I've been murder and police-free since arriving in France."

Aunt Beanie moved to stand behind Keya and Ryan. "Is it lovely there?"

"Heavenly," replied Dotty, smiling. "And now we're in May it's warm and the flowers are blooming, and we can enjoy family meals outside. Didier's mum is a marvellous cook. I'm learning so much."

Again Ryan cleared his throat before asking, "Do you know when you're coming back?"

Dotty looked down at Earl Grey as she stroked him. "Believe it or not, despite his French diet, he's losing weight. He's enjoying hunting in the barns and fields."

"He needed to," remarked Aunt Beanie.

Dotty looked up at them and admitted, "I'm not sure when I'll be back. I've agreed to stay here until the girls finish school and for the beginning of their summer holidays. The whole family is going away in August, so I've decided to," Dotty paused, "go to Edinburgh to see my parents. They recently moved to the city, and it's time I reconnected with them. Then I can move on."

"That sounds like an excellent idea," agreed Aunt Beanie. "And Edinburgh will be great in August with the Festival, but also busy and expensive. We thought it might help you out, and us, if Ryan moved into the cottage for a while. He's not finding it easy living back with his parents."

"That's a fantastic idea," enthused Dotty. "I wasn't sure what to do as I didn't want to give up the cottage until I knew what I was doing, but it would help a lot if I didn't have to pay all the rent."

"Excellent, then that's agreed," declared Aunt Beanie. "We'll speak again soon, but enjoy yourself in France, and in Edinburgh."

"Bye," chorused Keya, Ryan, Ozzie, Gilly, Dr Peter and Norman.

Just under two weeks later, Keya arrived at Akemans at half past eight in the morning for a site meeting. It was the first of June, and a bright sunny day. As Keya climbed out of her squad car, she glanced up at the honey-coloured stone walls of the antiques centre and smiled.

June was due to be a busy month with her sister's imminent wedding and, fingers crossed, the opening of the cafe. She was excited to see what work had been done since she'd had a brief look round the previous week after another busy auction at Akemans.

The metal fence was open and, as she entered the site, she wondered who had replaced Brad on the team. She no longer needed to negotiate wooden planks across areas of bare earth as stone paving slabs had been laid across the top section of landscaping. On the slope down to the river, patches of ground had been marked off with string and planted with grass seed.

She looked up at the brick walls of the extension, which looked complete. "We start on the roof today," remarked Vic Peters as he joined her beside the extension. "But come and look at the glass window. It turned out really well and will give customers a fantastic view of the waterwheel."

"Any idea when Rowan will install it?" asked Keya.

"He confirmed his team have completed most of the paddles and they're currently working on the structure. He's confident it'll be ready by the middle of June, but I'd allow an extra week. I know you've already delayed your opening, but hopefully we can give you early access to the mill and the extension so you can start fitting out."

"Wow, it's all coming together." Keya felt a nervous fluttering in her stomach.

"It certainly is. Come inside and we'll have a brew. I even bought you some Earl Grey tea bags."

Keya smiled. "Thank you. That's just what I need."

Darjeeling and A Deadly Disappearance

Can Keya open The Waterwheel Cafe in time? Will her sister's wedding proceed smoothly? Find out in this, the second book in The Waterwheel Cafe Mystery series.

A cancelled wedding. A runaway bride. Can a community police officer find the frightened fiancée before the church bells ring?

Claim Your Copy of Earl Grey and Shallow Graves at https://books2read.com/Darjeeling

Would you like to read Keya's first case with her friend Dotty? And discover how The Waterwheel Cafe and Dotty Sayers Antique Mystery series began?

Find out in the prequel, *Hour is Come,* when you sign up to my newsletter for updates at www.VictoriaTait.com.

Fake Death

Have you read the first book in the Dotty Sayers Antique Mystery series?

Young widow, Dotty Sayers, is delighted with her new auction house job in Britain's picturesque Cotswolds. But she's shocked by a soldier's death on Remembrance Day. She realises appearances can be deceiving, but can she track down the real culprit and prevent an innocent man from imprisonment?

Claim your copy of Fake Death at https://books2read.com/FakeDeath

If you enjoyed this book, please tell someone you know. And for those people you don't know, leave a review to help them decide whether or not to read it.

For more information visit VictoriaTait.com

KEYA'S NOTES - EARL GREY TEA

Earl Grey is a flowery black tea favoured by many English tea drinkers.

It has a floral, citrus aroma because it's flavoured with oil from the rind of the bergamot orange. This fruit is thought to be a cultivated hybrid blending the bitter Seville orange of the Mediterranean, with the sweet lime/lemon of Southeast Asia. I can taste the bitter note, which is why I prefer sweeter teas like Darjeeling.

As with many teas, aficionados believe it should be drunk without milk, which dulls its flavour, and if anything has to be added, it should be a slice of lemon, to maintain its crisp, sharp flavour.

The origin of Earl Grey, as with all teas, lies with the Chinese. They've been flavouring water with leaves for over 4,000 years. Over time, Chinese tea masters have experimented with different flavours, from jasmine flowers to rosebuds to sweet lychee fruits.

Earl Grey is named after Charles, 2nd Earl Grey, who was the British Prime Minister between 1830 and 1834. Although several brands lay claim to marketing the first Earl Grey tea, exactly how the earl was involved in its conception is debated.

The official version is that he received some as a diplomatic present and asked British tea merchants to recreate it.

Another, more romantic story which I prefer, is that a Chinese mandarin tea master blended the tea as a gift, and used bergamot as flavouring to offset the taste of lime in the well water at the Earl's estate, Howick Hall, in the Northeast of England.

It is said that Lady Grey loved the tea so much she used it exclusively when entertaining. London society followed her example, so she asked London tea merchants to recreate it.

There are variations on Earl Grey. Lady Grey, has additional lemon and Seville orange peel. French Earl Grey contains rose petals and Russian Earl Grey has lemongrass added.

Her Majesty Queen Elizabeth II enjoyed a cup of Earl Grey.

KEYA'S CHOCOLATE CHIP COOKIE RECIPE

Ingredients

240 gms 8.5 ozs 2 ¼ Sticks	Butter
150 gms 5.25 ozs 1 ½ Cups	Brown Sugar
200 gms 7 ozs 1 ½ Cups	Self Raising Flour
200 gms 7ozs 1 ¼ Cups	Chocolate Chips

(milk, dark white or combination)

Method

1. Set the oven to 180 °C/355 °F/Gas Mark 4.
2. Grease 2 baking sheets
3. Place the butter and sugar in a bowl and beat until soft and creamy.
4. Sieve the flour into the bowl and fold it into the mixture with a wooden spoon.
5. Add the chocolate chips and mix until it forms a rough ball.
6. Divide the mixture into two. Chill one half.
7. Flour your hands
8. With the remaining mixture, using a dessert spoon to take spoonfuls of it and roll them into golf ball sizes.
9. Place the golf balls on the baking trays leaving plenty of room between them to spread.

10. Flatten the golf balls slightly.
11. Bake for 12-15 minutes, or until golden brown.
12. Leave to stand for 5 minutes before placing them on a cooling rack.
13. Repeat with the second half of the mixture.

This recipe is so good you can swap the chocolate chips for oats, raisins and chopped apricots, or substitute some chocolate chips with cherries, cranberries, or chopped walnut or almonds.

As I know many of you reading this are from the US, I've tried to convert the quantities to ounces and cups, so I hope I have the measurements right.

I had to double the quantities to make this work, but do you know what's so great about this recipe? You can make half and freeze the other until friends announce they're popping round, when you defrost the mixture in the microwave, and cook and serve freshly baked cookies.

I hope you and your friends enjoy my chocolate chop cookies!

UNTITLED

Printed in Great Britain
by Amazon

62128636R00123